The Crystal Mouse

The Crystal Mouse

Babs H. Deal

Doubleday & Company, Inc.
Garden City, New York 1973

ISBN: 0-385-05875-6
Library of Congress Catalog Card Number 72–84903
Copyright © 1972, 1973 by the Babs H. Deal Family Trust
(Babs H. Deal, Trustee)
All Rights Reserved
Printed in the United States of America

For Bill and Mary Ann Heath

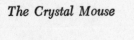

The Crystal Mouse

Chapter 1

It had rained at the cemetery; a soft thin drizzle from a thin cloud cover, but rain. Enough rain to turn the flowers soggy and to release the flat, yet acrid, smell of the fading hothouse blooms. Sara stood in the wet grass staring at a wilting chrysanthemum spray, feeling her heels sinking into the damp sandy soil, and tried not to look at the open grave.

A solicitous undertaker's assistant came to her with an opened umbrella and she stood under it staring now at the freckled hand holding the black handle. A part of her was distastefully amused because they had needed rain so badly. Everyone said so. All the time. And it took Howard dying to bring it down, she thought. It's as though he were a corn god, dying for the plants.

The thought of Howard, solid, plump, ordinary Howard, as a corn god was so incongruous she smiled involuntarily. Beside her, the freckled boy shifted uncomfortably.

Father Cartwright was mumbling over the grave, his black hair gleaming wetly in the drizzle, prayer book held firmly away from his nearsighted eyes. Too vain for glasses, she thought, and too new a minister to know it all by heart. She knew the prayer he was reading by heart. But she was old enough to have attended a lot of funerals. Though she hadn't expected to attend this one.

It didn't seem possible to her that she had outlived Howard. She had never considered that such a thing could happen. But obviously it had. The minister was beckoning her forward, and another assistant was holding out rose petals for her to drift into the grave. Howard's brother, Jack, was looking sternly at her through his bifocals. Howard's sister-in-law, Betty Jane, was crying.

She took the petals and released them over the grave.

"Well now," Jack said. "Well now."

Why must he say everything twice? she thought. He has said everything twice for thirty years.

He patted her awkwardly on the arm. "The car, the car," he said.

They trudged damply through the cemetery grass to the gravel drive and she let them put her into the mustiness of the car. She sat alone in the center of the back seat staring at Howard's and Betty Jane's backs.

"It's such a pity Howie couldn't get here," Betty Jane said. She turned around and looked at Sara, her plump face mournful as the sky. "I'll never understand why he had to go so far away to live. Or why you and Howard came here, for that matter."

"Now, now. None of that," Jack said.

"Or why you wouldn't bring him home," Betty Jane went on. "Nobody should be buried in Florida. It doesn't seem right."

"It is something we decided," Sara said.

She stared out the window at the road, clogged with traffic, the cars sliding by on the wet pavement, their windshield wipers whipping sluggishly back and forth.

"Then you are going to stay?" Betty Jane said.

"Of course, I'm going to stay," Sara said impatiently. "We bought the apartment. There is nothing at . . . home. We sold it all."

"You could get an apartment there," Betty Jane said stubbornly.

"I don't want an apartment there," Sara said.

Betty Jane subsided, leaving Sara to her headache and the sound of their windshield wipers and the burning eyes of the traffic lights punctuating the rain-slick highway.

She wondered why she always had a headache after the worst was over. It never came in time to incapacitate her for the terrible things she wanted to avoid doing. Only afterward, when the worst was done. She shut her eyes, remembering the terrible dash to the safety deposit box, with Howard lying dead in the half-empty apartment. She would never have, could never have, done it if she hadn't still felt he was alive and directing her. He had always been most insistent about that. *If I ever die before you, get to the bank. Get those things out of that box before probate. Get to the bank before you call the undertaker. Get to the bank.*

She hadn't known where the key was, couldn't remember, had had to take his keys, had almost wrecked the car on the causeway bridge. But she had done it, just as Howard had always told her, had managed somehow to look normal enough to sign the form and go into that little room like a grave itself and make the obscene double-key ritual with the brisk short safety-deposit woman. She'd even had enough sense to carry her biggest leather bag so that nothing showed when she came out.

She had driven back calmly enough because all the way her mind had been saying to Howard, "What would I have done if it hadn't been during banking hours? What would I have done then?"

It was only after she had let herself back into the apartment and seen him lying there on the carpet that she actually realized he wouldn't answer her. Not about that or about anything. Ever. She had put the bag down on the floor beside him and stood looking at him for what seemed a long time. Then she had gone out and found the caretaker. "My husband," she'd said. "I think he's had a heart attack."

Then there had been the doctor and the ambulance and the phone calls to Howie in New Zealand and Jack in Minnesota, and the lawyer, and the bank that held the trust. And the funeral home. She had done it all just the way Howard had told her it would have to be done if the time ever came. She hadn't had to think at all. But then suddenly it had been late in the afternoon and Jack and Betty Jane's plane not due until that night. The little apartment where they were staying until they could get completely moved into the new condominium was empty of everyone. It hadn't been time to eat. She had stood in the center of the room and looked around her. "But what do I do now, Howard?" she had said softly out loud. "What is it I do now?"

And it had seemed to her that she could hear his voice, brisk, impatient, exasperatedly explanatory. "I'd have a shot of whiskey, if I were you."

She'd had to bite her lip to keep from saying, "But, Howard, I don't *like* liquor very much."

It was only afterward, when Jack and Betty Jane were there filling the small apartment with their voices and grief, that it occurred to her that she could drink all the coffee she wanted now.

She stirred in the back seat of the car and took her eyes from the highway. "I'd like some coffee," she said.

"It really isn't good for you, is it?" Betty Jane said.

"No. Not according to Howard and the doctor," she said. "But that is what I want."

"Have you really given Sanka a try?" Betty Jane said.

"I don't like it," Sara said.

Betty Jane turned all the way around again and looked at her. "I really don't know who's going to look after you now," she said.

Sara looked back at her. "God?" she said.

That shut Betty Jane up again.

The apartment was dreary when they let themselves in and Sara went around turning on all the lamps before she plugged in the coffeepot.

This was the apartment in which she and Howard had spent the winters for more years than she remembered accurately. For as long as Howard had been successful enough to take two months off in the winter anyway. It was a pleasant enough place

4

for a two-month stay, a living room furnished with wicker and chintz, two small bedrooms, a hallway of a kitchen. She tried to brighten it each year with her own ash trays and towels and pillows, but it was obviously a place for transients. And now, with so many of their personal things already moved into the new condominium, it had become again something just this side of a motel room.

"I think I'll stay in the new apartment tonight," Sara said.

There was a pregnant silence broken only by the comforting thunk of the coffeepot.

She smiled. "You did say you had to catch the plane back tonight, didn't you?" she said. "I don't want to stay here alone. It would be better in the new place."

Betty Jane looked at Jack. He shrugged and she sighed loudly. "We were still hoping you'd change your mind and come on back to Minneapolis with us," she said. "Just for a week or so anyway."

Sara shook her head. "I've got to get used to being alone," she said. "That would only put it off."

"But is the new apartment in any shape to stay in?" Betty Jane said.

"Oh yes. There are crates and boxes unpacked still, but the basic furniture's there. No drapes, but that hardly matters that many floors up, does it?"

"I guess not," Betty Jane said doubtfully.

"I'll get the coffee," Sara said.

They sat around the blond maple coffee table, sipping from the kitchen cups she hadn't moved yet. "It's so strange," Sara said. "You'd think this happened because of all the moving. But, of course, it didn't. Howard was awfully insistent we hire every bit of it done. Because of *my* heart. We were going to do the fixing up ourselves, but we hadn't even started that. All he'd done for a couple of days was sit around drinking bourbon and helping eat up the food so we wouldn't have to move that."

Her in-laws looked at her uneasily.

5

"He was just sitting there," Sara said. "Having a drink and looking at the *TV Guide.*"

"Don't think about it," Jack said. "It doesn't help to think about it."

"Would you rather have a drink, Jack?" Sara said.

"Well, maybe I would, maybe I would," he said. "Don't get up, I'll fix it."

"I'll get it," she said. She opened the kitchen cabinet and looked at the row of bottles. "Scotch?"

"On the rocks," he said.

"Betty Jane?"

"Oh no."

She made the drink and brought it to her brother-in-law. "I really feel as though you shouldn't have tried to make the trip," she said. "It's going to be miserable flying half the night or sitting around O'Hare and then having to go to work tomorrow."

"Don't be ridiculous, Sara," Betty Jane said. "I just wish you'd come back with us. I'd stay here, but I have to teach."

"I know," Sara said. "I told you I'll be all right."

"I wish you'd stay here though," Betty Jane said. "You don't even have your TV in over there."

"All those arrangements will give me something to do."

She felt sorry for her in-laws. They'd never been close, to either her or Howard, and she knew they'd be very relieved to get on that flight to the Midwest tonight, bad weather at home or not. She wondered suddenly if they'd been expecting to get anything in the will. But surely they knew Howard better than that. He had loaned Jack money on at least two occasions and never gotten it back, and she was quite sure he'd told Jack that was his share of whatever he happened to leave. There really hadn't been all that much anyway, not tied up the way it was in the trust fund and the new apartment. Still, they might have thought . . .

"Is there anything of Howard's you'd like to have, Jack?" she said. "Besides the watch and studs. I know he wanted you to have them."

It wasn't true, but she felt slightly embarrassed because it wasn't.

"Oh no, no, Sara," Jack said. "I didn't expect even that."

"Well . . . there's all the fishing gear."

"Don't think about that stuff now," he said gruffly. "You've got enough on your mind."

It occurred to her that Jack was really a very nice man. She just didn't know him very well. She didn't, at the moment, seem to know anybody very well. The thought startled her. Of course I do, she told herself. There's . . . But she didn't know who there was.

Her family were all long since dead. These two people sitting here were what was left of Howard's. Her son and his wife were half a world away in a ridiculous land where she didn't even want to go for a visit. There was Howard's partner, but he was just that—Howard's partner, retired now too in Miami, and his wife who—well, was his wife, not Sara's friend. There had been Moira, but she was dead. So many of the old friends *were* dead. And had there ever been that many anyway?

Nonsense, Sara thought. There have always been people around us. It's just that here in Florida we were transients. There was always Howard, of course. But Howard is gone.

She got up and went to refill her coffee cup. Looking out the kitchen window she saw that the rain had stopped. The sun was streaking through the cloud cover and she knew it would be completely fair by sunset. "I suppose everyone is going to be disappointed," she said. "It really didn't rain enough to help anything after all." She tried to smile to ease the worry on her guests' faces. "Well, at least I don't have any plants to worry about," she said. "The building people take care of all that. They really take care of everything. I'm very lucky I have a place like that to go."

She knew that she was. She had been completely against the thought of a condominium at first, but that was before she saw the model and realized how roomy it was. It would be infinitely better than this apartment and in reality better than the house in Minneapolis with the increasing worry about the pipes and the furnace and the driveway in winter. The house that had become more and more of a burden as the years passed.

Howard had bought the condominium apartment before the first stake had been driven into the ground to build the structure. It was all a part of his plan and method for making things work in their declining years. He had become very big on that the last year or so. But she had never thought it would make any difference to her. She'd always been so sure he would outlive her.

During the previous year they had watched the building going up on the outlying key. Howard's final retirement had given them more time than they'd ever had together, but it had been filled with the move, with the business transactions necessary: selling the Minneapolis house, transferring funds, because, Howard said, Florida was still the cheapest state to die in, shopping for the new things they'd need for the new place, selling the old things there wouldn't be any room for in the new one.

Howard had been very good about what he'd let her keep, the few really good pieces of furniture and all her crystal collection. She had started it years ago when Howie was a baby, and it had given her pleasure for all the years since. At first all the objects had been small, but later, when there had been more money, Howard had gotten her some really good Steuben glass. There was quite a lot of it now, and she had been happy to see that the new apartment had a wall of built-in bookcases that would house it. It was over there now, still packed in excelsior, waiting its place on the new white shelves. Maybe tonight she'd unpack it. It would fill the time before bedtime.

The condominium was called the Triton. It was twelve stories high, standing starkly back from a strip of beach. The landscaping was recent and it still looked raw and new, tended grass amid concrete. There was a swimming pool, as yet unfilled, and parking facilities underneath the building. It was very isolated, but a second one was to go up next to it within the foreseeable future. There had been others, closer to town, but Howard had said this one had the best view. Though, actually, she thought, he preferred it because it had been the best deal in terms of cash outlay. There had been some sort of retirement benefit thing that had enabled them to get one of the best apartments for the price of one of the less-desirable ones. She didn't really understand the contract. Howard had always taken care of that sort of thing, but she wished now that she had read it herself. She guessed she'd have to.

At any rate there was now immediate occupancy. It was finished, after what had seemed to her an interminable time abuilding. They had been planning to finish moving in this week.

The thought of the building was comforting to her. There would be a doorman and other people around her. It wouldn't be like this apartment, an isolated cottage in a block of cottages which were sometimes rented, sometimes not, with the landlord always difficult to find and cajole. Surely the condominium contract would take care of the cajoling for her. They had said, too, that there would be a resident nurse, perhaps, and there were to be social rooms and shuffleboard and the pool. She didn't particularly look forward to any of these activities, but it would be good to know that they were there. There would be people around her, laughing, playing, enjoying a new kind of life.

She felt grateful to Howard for having provided her this place to go in this moment of need. It was so like him. Consistency. At least in the mechanics of life.

She insisted on driving Jack and Betty Jane to the airport, though they were reluctant. They stood together in the glassed waiting room watching the other travelers until the plane was called. She walked them to the barrier gate and saw them climb awkwardly aboard. She started to sit down on the stone bench to wait for the plane to take off, but it occurred to her that she did not have to do that. She hated it, but she had always done it if she were in an airport small enough. Waited, patiently, but fearfully, watching the gasoline truck and the baggage truck, and the laughing boys in their Mickey Mouse sound helmets. Seeing

9

the pilot talking to the ground through his microphone, hearing the motors revved for testing and then finally for taxiing; seeing the red light begin to flash at last and the stairs go up. She could never actually watch the plane take off, preferring to watch its reflection in the plate glass of the terminal. But she had always stayed to the bitter end, until the trail of black kerosene smoke was only a wisp high up and away, and whoever she had been seeing off was gone irrevocably into another world. Betty Jane and Jack wouldn't care whether she waited fearfully or not. She could go on home. Still she hesitated; then, firming her mind, walked back through the terminal to her car, thinking of the times she had put Howard or Howie on a jet and watched them disappear. A small morbid thought crossed her mind. Howard had now done just that; disappeared swiftly and completely into another world, only this time never to return, this time not even leaving that wisp of black smoke in the sky to show the way he'd gone.

Stop it, she told herself. Just stop it. You have not only tonight but a long time to get through. Some superstitious corner of her mind seemed to tell her that with Howard's death a longer life than she'd bargained for had been insured her. She did not want to think at all about what she would do with it. For now there was only the job of getting the pieces of crystal onto a newly painted shelf.

The car was a new Galaxie. For many years they'd had two cars, Howard's sports car, usually a Mercedes, and her car, usually a compact, an English Ford or a Mustang. But with retirement Howard had decided sports cars weren't practical. They would only need one car and it should be a sensible car, one for either local traffic or the road. She unlocked it and got behind the wheel, missing the feel of her own small car with its touch of foreignness, not enough to make her uncomfortable or to make parts hard to find, but different enough to make it her own. This one never had been and never would be. It hadn't been Howard's either.

But, typically, she didn't think of the possibility of trading, of getting back her small car. The decision had been made. For her.

The Galaxie was part of her inherited life-plan, put into effect by Howard, now having to be utilized.

It was almost sunset and she drove slowly from the airport into town. The sunsets were strange, due to the lack of rain and the dust in the atmosphere. The sun, an angry red ball, dropped slowly toward the horizon, then disappeared before it got there, going under the bank of dark haze caused, some said, by the brush fires of a dry country. Others said it was the pollution from the plants to the north of this resort area. Whatever the cause, it had a depressing effect. The night, when it came, seemed total. As the sun sank she began to drive more rapidly, anxious to get back to the lighted apartment and the job of moving. The intricacies of moving seemed a kind of medicine, needed and welcome.

But in the driveway of the small cottage she felt tired suddenly, depleted by the funeral and the responsibility of Jack and Betty Jane. She longed for a hot bath and bed. She unlocked her door slowly, glad she had left the lamps on, sorry for the silence. She crossed the room and turned on the TV, but the sudden blast of sound, a cheerful, unrelenting voice telling her about the Now Generation, was worse than the silence. She switched it off and stood indecisively in the middle of the room. She was almost sorry not to be on the plane north with Jack and Betty Jane, eating the pre-prepared meal, watching the sky outside, feeling invulnerable for once in an airplane because of the twisted fate that was granting her a new—and possibly unwanted—life.

She could hear the clock ticking in the kitchen and the hum of the refrigerator and the occasional clunk from the toilet tank.

She crossed the room and picked up the phone book, idly flipping through the pages. Surely there was someone she could call to come for coffee. Her mind slid back to the funeral, the pitifully few people in the small Episcopal chapel. There had been the maid, dressed in black with an enormous hat of black flowers. There had been the landlord of the small complex of apartments here. There had been several couples she remembered vaguely from cocktail parties. There had been the lawyer and the trust man from the bank. There had been a restaurant owner and, oddly enough, the man to whom Howard had sold his Mercedes.

She put down the phone book.

From outside she could hear the swish of water as the caretaker turned on the sprinklers for the evening watering. There were restrictions on yard watering and it could only be done between seven and nine. After dark. The reminder made her glad again of the tended condominium. She went briskly to the kitchen and dumped and rinsed the coffeepot and put it into an empty cardboard box. She added cups and saucers, coffee and spoons and the few things from the refrigerator, milk and sweet rolls and some cheese and bread.

She took her gown and robe from behind the bathroom door, averting her eyes from Howard's robe, still hanging on the hook, and her slippers from under the bed. She found an unread magazine and carried it all out to the car.

She came back in and stood hesitantly in the middle of the room, frowning. Then she took a bottle of California sherry from the cabinet, and, impulsively, a carton of cigarettes from the bedside table. She hadn't smoked in years, but it seemed to her in the moment that they should be included in the night's emergency cache. She turned out the lights and locked the door and got into the alien automobile.

The town of Cape Haze was having its evening rush hour as residents and tourists went out to early dinner. She drove through the stream of traffic, her lights dimmed, frowning at the oncoming headlight glare. To her left the city marina lights reflected bluely in the still waters of the bay and for a moment she considered stopping and having dinner in the marina restaurant. She could look out over the water at the boats and listen to people talking and the sounds of silver and china clinking. Then she thought of coming back to the car alone, later, and drove on. She wasn't hungry anyway. She knew she should eat, but she hadn't been able to, not in—how many days now? Three?

At the phone booth on the corner two boys were scuffling in the light from the booth. They were laughing and calling obscene remarks to each other, the words easily recognizable above the sound of the traffic. She shivered and drove on to the intersection for the turn to the bridge.

Waiting for the green arrow she was faced with the bulk of a new motel, a towering ugly block topped by a steer's head, the enormous horns seeming to clutch the windows of the tackily balconied rooms below. What is a steer doing presiding like a Texan over a Florida intersection? she thought. And her mind threw up a picture of LBJ, glasses on the end of his nose.

A honking behind her made her realize the light had changed and she turned left toward the bridge, thinking, I really must eat something. LBJ, indeed. Howard had voted the straight Republican ticket all his life, even though he had known HHH personally. She hadn't always. But that was her own secret. The musty green of the voting booth curtains did provide a certain security for personal aberrations in a too-certain world.

She had voted for JFK. Approaching the bridge, she smiled to herself for the first time since the corn-god thought of afternoon. She might even have voted for RFK. She liked Ethel and all those children. But she was afraid of some things. Those boys in their tight pants and sandals and long hair, scuffling at the phone booth. In the event, of course, she hadn't had to decide.

She slowed down for the bridge. It was a four-lane bridge, with a high draw, and most people considered it only an extension of the highway. For that reason there had been some terrible accidents on it, cars ricocheting off the center barrier and over the edge, cars piling up at the exits. She had sat for hours one day halfway across the causeway approach while the police grappled with a six-car accident and divers tried to rescue the trapped victims who had gone over. She drove across it slowly and carefully, anxious not to hang a wheel against the curbing.

Once across the bridge the driving was easier. There was a straight stretch and then the small shopping circle with its lights and the sound of rock from a bar. She thought that she'd have to get to know this circle better, because it would probably be where she would be doing most of her shopping. She had never used it very much when they lived on the mainland. Downtown had been handy. Downtown would now be all the way back across the bridge.

She drove off the circle and across a humpbacked bridge and dropped suddenly into darkness and silence. The traffic had ceased, the sounds had ceased. Tall casuarinas nodded at her from the roadside; stars, released from neon, sprang into being in the sky.

She rounded a curve, hit the straightaway, and increased her speed. She passed an empty golf course, the sound of spraying water drenching the greens, falling around her like a blanket. She passed a shack that sold fishing gear, its lone light raying into the darkness, shadowy shapes around it with lines and poles and the gleam of beer cans raised in the darkness. Everything seemed strange and somehow threatening. She told herself that the fishermen were all someone like Howard, intent merely on catching a fish. A slimy, wet, cold creature from another world to bring home and plop majestically onto their wives' clean sink, the reek of fish permeating the houses and apartments, the gleam of triumph in the catch proclaiming them victors of the universe, the flaccid dead thing in the sink to be dealt with by the female. That made her feel better. She looked at the dark fishermen shapes with understanding. Her uneasiness vanished. Ahead she saw the lights of the towering condominium.

The building looked just as her imaginings had told her: solid, big, comforting in the night. The twelve stories stretched skyward with a red warning light on top to ward off airplanes. A row of gleaming lights stretched up the outside of the building in a fine unwavering line from bottom floor to top. A line of round-globed lights lit up the approach to the entry, banishing darkness. She turned, almost happily, into the globe-lined drive.

The night watchman came outside at the sound of her car. He

wore the comforting garb of the lawman, a billed cap, serviceable blue shirt and pants, a pistol in a holster on his fat hip. He was gray haired and red faced and very ordinary and familiar. He approached the car. He touched his cap.

"Why, good evening, Mrs. Hillstrom," he said. "Didn't expect you out here tonight. I'm real sorry to hear about Mr. Hillstrom. Real sorry."

There *he* goes, saying things twice like Jack, she thought. It's some kind of tick.

"I wanted to come on out for the night, Mr. Bishop," she said. "I didn't want to stay in the old apartment."

"You mean you want to move right on in?"

"Yes."

"Well . . . sure, fine," he said. "Do you remember the number of your parking slot?"

"It's the same as the apartment, isn't it?" she said brightly. "Twelve B?"

"That's right," he said. "Just drive on in here and up the ramp."

She drove into the parking entrance. There were lights here too, dots of brightness in the midst of gray concrete. The ramp went upward around arched supports, blank walls facing one at each turning. It was, she thought, like being inside the Colosseum. She had never been inside the Colosseum—traveling extensively had been one of the things they were going to do in these declining years—but she had seen movies of the inside of the Colosseum. She had seen movies, too, of the inside of parking ramps. They had not been good movies. What is the matter with me? she thought. I seem to keep having bad thoughts. But then, of course, it is the day of a funeral. It is the day of *Howard's* funeral. The sentence seemed to have no reality for her. She didn't believe it at all. What she believed was the stark gray of the parking ramp, and the strange and frightening fact that there was not one single car anywhere in the vast subterranean space.

She drove on, up and around, beginning to feel as though she were on some celestial escalator from which there was no escape.

Then her lights flashed onto 12 B and she parked the car. For a moment, in the silence after she switched off her motor, she sat staring at the blank wall in front of her. Then she hurriedly looked into the back seat. It was nonsensical. She had looked into the back seat before she got into the car. She always looked into the back seat because once, years ago, when they were young—very young—Moira, her best friend, had told her about the time her boy friend had hidden on the floor of the back seat of her car and suddenly raised up, frightening her to death and almost causing her to have a wreck. The boy friend had not lasted long as a boy friend after that, but he had served as a cautionary tale to Moira's whole circle of girl friends. None of them ever got into an empty car at night again without carefully looking into the back seat. One of them, a bright happy girl named Constance Clary, had kept an umbrella in the car with which she poked energetically behind her before she even looked. So now, though the looking was redundant, she did it anyway. There was only her cardboard box of supplies, a discarded Coke bottle, and a battered city map. She switched off her lights, pulled up the emergency brake, and got the cardboard box out of the back seat.

There was a lighted doorway near the parking slot and she could see the night watchman standing inside holding a bunch of keys. She went to the door and he let her into a carpeted hallway with a bank of elevators. He took the box from her and punched the elevator button.

He rode up with her in the elevator, holding the box gingerly in front of him. She tried to think of something to say to him, but her mind was blank. She stared instead at the buttons in front of her and wondered what would happen if she pushed Emergency.

The doors slid open with a whisper and they stepped into the carpeted hallway, gray carpet with lighter gray walls, lights running the length of the silent closed corridor. He marched to the door at the end, set back within an angle, with 12 B in discreet black letters. He set down her box and asked her for her key.

She was startled and fumbled in her purse in embarrassment. He took the key from her, opened the door, and reached his hand inside to turn on the light. She stared at his bunch of keys, wondering what sort of delicacy made him ask for hers when he was obviously carrying the passkey.

He set her box down inside the door. "The air conditioning is on," he said. "We leave it on to protect the apartments from mold and such. But you might need to turn it up. If you need anything, just buzz on the intercom."

"Thank you, Mr. Bishop," she said. She wanted to ask him to wait while she checked the apartment, but she realized that would sound silly. It had been firmly locked since the last time she and Howard had been up with a load of boxes.

He said good night, touched his cap, and went away toward the elevator, his gun bumping on his ample hip.

For just a moment she left the door open between herself and the comforting presence of Mr. Bishop's back at the elevator. Then he entered the sliding doors and was gone, and she quickly locked and shut her door and fastened the chain against the empty corridor. She picked up her box and went toward her unused kitchen, turning on wall switches as she went.

The apartment had the faint dead cooled-air smell of air conditioning. Though it was only late April it was muggy outside from the small shower of afternoon and she was glad of the conditioned air. She put her box on the kitchen table and made a quick inspection of the apartment, including the closets. Then she walked across the empty expanse of living room carpet and looked out the window at her exclusive and expensive view.

The apartment faced onto the Gulf of Mexico. In the light of the globed lamps that ringed the empty swimming pool below she could see the edge of surf, banging regularly onto the strip of beach that edged the landscaped grounds of the building.

She turned off the living room light and came to look again. Now, from the darkness, she could see the stars, and a second line of white far away in the Gulf where the surf was breaking on a sand bar. The pool lights below seemed an intrusion on the oceanic peace before her. But a part of her was glad of them.

She turned from the window and went briskly into the clean new kitchen to prepare and plug in her coffeepot. While it thunked cheerfully away she went into the bedroom and put clean sheets from the already stocked linen closet on her twin bed. Except for the mechanical company of the electrical appliance the apartment was very still around her, and in the act of plumping her pillow a disturbing thought came to her. She could see in her mind's eye the building as she had driven toward it, and she realized that the line of lights from top to bottom that had seemed so cheerful was nothing more than the line of lights for the elevator shafts.

She stood, staring down at the blue roses on her pillow slip, a frozen feeling in the pit of her stomach, and thought of her solitary light streaking out of the apartment into the empty night.

The coffeepot finished its cycle and cut off with a last gentle rumble. "There weren't any cars in the parking space either," she said aloud, and the sound of her voice seemed to echo through all of the building around her. A building designed for sixty-five families, and housing herself and a night watchman twelve empty, spacious, stories below.

Chapter 2

"This is silly," she said, and finished making the bed with neat quick movements. Then she made herself cross the bedroom and go to the kitchen and make a cheese sandwich. She poured coffee into one of the cups she'd brought and her hand trembled, sloshing it onto the pristine countertop. She searched vaguely around the room before she remembered where she'd put the paper towels, feeling panicky at the thought of the coffee staining the brand-new Formica. She mopped it up and felt immediately better as though she had performed some terribly necessary duty, and that They, whoever They might be, would award her a gold star for the center of her forehead as for memorizing ten verses about Paul in Sunday school.

She sat down at her new kitchen table and ate the sandwich and drank the coffee. I never did like Paul, she thought. That was one of the good things about becoming an Episcopalian with Howard. I could forget all that stuff about Paul. Paul, writing his interminable letters to all those bored people in the outland churches, elevating himself to the role of New Savior, giving women a hard time, begging for money in a way that would have made Jesus of Nazareth take a whip to *him*.

She felt so bold with the unaccustomed thought that she opened the carton of cigarettes and tore open a package and lit one. It tasted strong and harsh and strange, but immeasurably comforting. So much for you, Howard, she thought, and felt immediately the wrongness of the words. She'd meant to say, So much for you, Paul. She had a moment of strong guilt and almost said out loud, I'm sorry, Howard. But she caught herself in time, knowing she wouldn't want to hear the sound of her own voice again in the silence of the empty apartment.

She got up and washed her cup and saucer and plate and put away the food. Tomorrow, she thought, staring at the empty shelves, I'll have to stock the refrigerator. I will go to that interesting-looking store I saw on the circle. It will be fun. And I'm not going to start talking to Howard in my mind. I am not going to say, Yes, Howard, it's an expensive store, but I'll only be buying a very few things, just for me.

She left the kitchen light on and went into her living room and stood staring at what was going to be her home for the rest of her life. It was a pretty room. There was a soft gray carpet, shades darker than the walls. The woodwork was white with a slight glow. The sofa and chairs, a nice blue, were already in place near the windows, her beautiful antique dining table was in its alcove with the ladderback chairs around it. The drapes, being made at Haralsons, would be a muted print of blues and greens. She had wanted pink, but Howard couldn't stand pink. Only the empty windows, awaiting those drapes, and the packing cases in the middle of the room gave a feeling of impermanence.

She went to the largest packing case and knelt and began to try to unfasten the stapling bands around it. They were much harder to manage than she had thought and she broke a fingernail. She sat down on the carpet and stared at it, feeling tears welling up behind her eyes. Don't start crying, Sara, she told herself. Go to the kitchen and find something to open the box. She got up and rummaged through Howard's neat tool drawer until she found a wire clipper and was able to open the crate with a feeling of triumph.

The crystal had all been neatly packed in excelsior by the moving people. She looked around for a newspaper and realized there wasn't one in the apartment. She'd have to have the address changed. That was one of a dozen things they'd been going to do this next week. She plunged her hands recklessly into the box and took out the first piece of crystal, letting the excelsior fall onto the carpet. It was her crystal mouse, the oldest and smallest piece of glass, that she had personally packed on top. She brushed him off and held him on the palm of her hand. He was delicate and cunning, pointed ears iridescent, curling tail a thin coil of fragility over his haunches. She took him carefully across the room and placed him in the exact center of the middle shelf where he sat looking back at her from a solitude as immense as her own.

She remembered the day she had first seen him, sitting on a piece of black velvet in the window of Dayton's department store. He had been all alone there too, a small gleaming extravagance that she had fallen in love with, standing on a cold blustery street, wrapped in the first fur coat Howard had ever given her. A fur coat that she hated.

"I didn't know I hated that coat," she said now to the mouse. "I had no idea before this moment that that was the reason I had to buy you."

The mouse stared back at her, crystal nose seeming to twitch and wiggle fine-drawn crystal whiskers, making Sara's own nose twitch involuntarily in response.

"I ought to dust you," she said. And made the long trip to the kitchen for a dustcloth.

There was a window over the kitchen sink, but she couldn't see out of it. Sara was a short woman and though she stood on tiptoe there was nothing in the window but darkness. She hesitated, then drew a chair up and stood on it and looked out. The kitchen window faced the side of the building and though the lights from the front and rear cast a small glow she couldn't distinguish anything. She had thought the shuffleboard court was on that side, but perhaps it wasn't lighted tonight. She gazed downward, trying to see the lines and markers in the darkness twelve stories below, but there was nothing. She climbed down and went back to dust her mouse and reset him carefully in his place of honor.

She worked steadily for what seemed to her a long time. Piece after piece of the crystal came up from the depths of excelsior and took its place on the shelves: the swan and the unicorn, the giraffe and the twinned gazelles, the Viking ship in full sail against the wind, the ugly frog and the lovely singing sword. All the animals and myths in frozen silicone, the fragile extravagance of beauty that had bested the snows of Minnesota and would best the sands of Florida.

The two boxes were empty and she sat back on her heels in the midst of the excelsior to look at her pregnant shelves. She glanced at her watch, feeling she had earned her bed. The small jeweled hands pointed unbelievably to nine minutes after nine.

She held her wrist to her ear and shook it, then looked again at the watch. The small second hand was sweeping majestically around the tiny white face. It was running.

Maybe it stopped for just a while, she thought. I'll turn on the radio and check.

She stood up, brushing the clinging bits of straw from her skirt, and crossed the expanse of gray carpet to her bedroom. The bedside lamp threw a small circle of light into the room and beside it the white radio looked cheerful, a link to the outside world. Another silly thought, she told herself. I'm really going to have to take myself in hand. You get in such a habit, over the years, of saying out loud to another person all those small and unimportant, even irrelevant, words that jump into your mind.

She turned the dial and heard the raucous voice of a native Texan telling her that Tammy Wynette had a reputation for being kind to other singers who were just getting started in the business. Because, Tammy said, others had been kind to her. Who is Tammy Wynette? Sara thought. And was answered by a sad sad voice singing "Don't Touch Me."

Her mind brought up a picture of Jesus of Nazareth, white robes flowing, standing on sandaled feet with the rocks behind him, warding off Mary with that stern gentle look. *Noli me tangere.* Jesus the Carpenter, and a kind girl named Tammy Wynette.

She sat on the edge of the bed and waited out the song. Then the announcer came again and told her it was eight-fifteen in Dallas. Her watch hadn't stopped at all. It was just that time was running slow now, running slow probably from now on.

I'll clean up the mess, she thought. She left the radio murmuring through the open bedroom door and took a broom and dustpan to the clinging straw in her living room, filling the empty new garbage can with it, setting the empty crates beside it for disposal in another day.

On her last trip to the kitchen she realized that she was listening. Listening for the sound, above the murmuring radio, of cars coming in, of someone coming home.

She laughed at herself with the realization. She couldn't possibly hear them this far from the ground. A hundred people could have come home to the Triton for the night and she would never have known it. She felt their presence then around her, closed into their own cubicles on the floors below, and was warmed by the thought. She poured more coffee and took it to her front windows. She switched out the living room lights and sat on her new blue couch and looked out at the Gulf of Mexico, wondering who else on the floors below was looking out at the same wide scene of sea and night.

When she finished the coffee she tiptoed to the window and looked out. There were no lights raying out below her. Only the same glow from the globed pool lights. I will go out on my balcony, she thought.

The balconies were one of the main selling points of the Triton, one for each apartment, small but usable, iron grillwork around them, the view in front. One for each and every apartment, insuring fresh air and salt air, insuring a sunset view, bespeaking luxury and health and exclusiveness.

The front windows of the living room were really doors, sliding glass panels leading onto the balcony. She stood looking at the latch, trying to remember if and how they locked. There was a round gold sticker in the middle of each sliding door to let the unwary know when they were shut. They met in the middle with an ordinary catch. She put her hand on the round handle and pulled and the door opened noiselessly on its new runners. She jumped back, startled. Was it possible the doors didn't lock at all?

She leaned over and examined the catch in the dim light from outside. There was a thumb lock, but it hadn't been on. She pushed the door on back and stepped onto her balcony. She and Howard had equipped it with two chairs, a table, and a small settee in white wrought iron. She stood in the middle of the small space, feeling crowded by the furniture, and looked right and left. To the right there was another balcony, dark and shadowy and a good hundred feet away. To her left there was only the corner of the building. Two balconies to the front side, two apartments, and no light from the other one.

She walked to the railing and looked down. Far below, the empty pool stared up at her like a rectangular eye. She leaned out and down. No light came from any window to ray out into space. She stood still, her hands gripping the railing, and listened. There were no sounds in the silence. She strained her ears and something came to her, a faint murmur. Perhaps it was from the apartment next door. They had come in and gone to bed while she worked and were now talking in the darkness. She nodded happily and went back inside, carefully pushing the latch up on the sliding doors. She knew there was no real need. It would take a human fly to get onto her balcony. But she locked it anyway.

It was only after she'd turned back into the apartment, thinking of lighting another cigarette from the pack in the kitchen, that she realized the murmur of voices came from her own radio left on in the bedroom.

She refused to be frightened by the awareness. She lit her cigarette boldly and drew on it, inhaling this time, feeling the smoke in her lungs with childish glee. At her age it really hardly mattered whether she had lung cancer or not. It probably didn't even matter that she was alone.

She went to the bathroom, determined to take a long luxurious bath. She turned on the taps, acting as though she had taken baths in this apartment for years. The water sputtered for a moment, ran indecisively, then settled down to a strong stream. While the tub filled she got her gown and robe from the cardboard box and laid them on the new wicker hamper. She found soap in the cupboard and unwrapped the new bar, placing it in the pretty shell soap fixture. She selected the largest, fluffiest white towel in the cupboard—the one Howard would usually choose—and draped it on the rack. Each movement seemed to her unique and distinct. She undressed slowly, only at the last moment turning to look at her body in the full-length mirror on the bathroom door.

For a moment she was startled by the image of herself. She had been feeling terribly old and used up and therefore invulnerable to fate. The body in the mirror wasn't quite that old.

She had always had a good figure, even though she'd never made anything of it, feeling embarrassed in anything tight or the least suggestive of showing off that figure. She had worn shirtwaists for years. The dress she'd just taken off was a shirtwaist, though black and of an expensive material. Now, released from the tacky style, her body was embarrassingly good; small breasts still firm, narrow waist, flat hips. There were dimples in the thighs, of course, and a few broken veins on her lower abdomen and flanks. The original firmness of muscle had drooped slightly with the years, but it still wasn't the body of an old woman, and the fast of the last few days had eliminated the few extra pounds she'd had around her waist. The sight of her body annoyed her. Women in their fifties should not have bodies anyone would want to look at. The idea seemed faintly obscene to her. She turned quickly from her image, turned off the water, and stepped into her tub.

She leaned back, prepared to have the water wash over her, relaxing the tensions of the day. Her eye fell on the pile of black clothing in the middle of the blue bathrug. She stepped out of the soothing bath and bundled it together and stuffed it into the hamper. She stepped back into the tub. The water had cooled off faintly and she turned the hot-water tap to warm it up. The tub was very full now and she leaned back, her head with its neat pepper-and-salt topknot propped on the rim of the tub. She willed her body to relax. Baths had always been one of her secret solutions to life, and she could feel the hot water beginning to supply its usual benison. She closed her eyes.

There was a sudden sound. Her eyes opened, focused in a shortsighted stare on the water faucets in front of her. She was aware that her body had tightened into a knot of apprehension. The sound of the radio still murmured at her from the adjoining bedroom, still playing country music. It had been something else that she had heard. She couldn't place the direction from which it had come.

She tensed and waited, but the sound didn't come again. It had been very slight and in the moment completely unidentifiable. It was a sound she was quite sure she wouldn't have heard at all if she had not been alone in the empty and unused apartment. It was probably then a sound normal to daily life, a sound she should have been able to place and ignore instantly. Except that she couldn't. Her whole body seemed concentrated on that one small sound and the possible source of it. She realized that she was holding herself perfectly still in the tub and that she had ceased to breathe. Still, the sound didn't come again.

In that moment of complete bodily stasis her mind began to

throw up images, images she hadn't known were in her mind, or certainly hadn't known she had brought into this apartment with her tonight.

The first was of some forgotten newspaper story of an ax murderer. He had killed, and killed again, and he had in desperation finally scrawled on the wall above a victim, in the victim's blood, a plea for help. PLEASE STOP ME. *Don't touch me.* Her mind supplied a newspaper picture of the blood scrawl. It was over a bathtub, crude letters on a tile wall. There is nobody in this apartment, she told herself. You latched the doors and checked it all yourself. The second image was from TV. A man had thrown a radio into the tub with his intended victim and electrocuted him in the bath.

She let her breath out slowly, trying to do it as quietly as possible. The bathroom door was open and she willed herself to turn around and look at the opening. But she couldn't do it. Instead, with a no-nonsense air that was nonetheless an action of complete panic, she picked up the soap and bathed herself as hurriedly and thoroughly as possible. It was a ritual, done in haste and fear and mindless panic, but with a primitive impulse behind it, telling her that if she bathed first before she leaped from the tub and went in search of that minute sound all would be well and she would be the victim only of her own imaginings, not of some real and true male entity with an ax.

She stepped out of the tub and roughly toweled herself dry and slipped into her robe. She made a gesture toward unstopping the bathtub and knew she was afraid of the sound of water running noisily out of the drain, betraying her to that nameless noise.

She stepped quietly to the door and looked around the frame. The bedroom looked just as it had when she left it, the bed lamp cozily on, the bed turned cozily down, the radio singing of a truck on the highway.

She crossed the room quietly and went into the hall. She went to the kitchen, she looked in the pantry, she came back out and looked around the living room. Then she steeled herself and opened all the closets. In a last gesture of foolishness and fear she half laughingly looked under the beds.

There was nothing but silence. She went to the bathroom and unstopped the tub. Then above the sound of water rushing unimpeded through the drains toward a ground far below, she heard the sound again and knew what it was; the air conditioning changing pitch as the thermostat regulated it.

The relief was so sudden and so complete that it sapped her. She could feel the slackness of muscle, the actual release of brain tension. She began to tremble, long shuddering tremors vying with long shuddering breaths. "Good heavens," she said aloud.

She went to sit on the edge of her blue-rosed bed, gripping both elbows with opposite hands until the trembling subsided. Then in a long-used and accustomed gesture of self-comfort she grasped her right wrist with her left hand. Like a child sucking its thumb, she thought. I wonder why I do it?

Moira had sat on her French provincial couch one day a million years ago and said, crossing her legs and lighting a cigarette, "Sara, darling, you're developing a tick. I wouldn't mention it, only you do it more and more. You hang onto your wrist like a swimmer saving himself from drowning. I know your wrists are beautiful, dear, but it really isn't a becoming thing to do. It makes you look a little desperate."

Moira had never looked desperate in her life. Sara had often wondered if she'd ever felt that way. She had been so tall and cool and self-possessed, her hazel eyes measuring the world and finding it wanting, but refusing to be disconcerted by that finding. If Moira were here now she would say, "Well, dear, we've looked everywhere, haven't we? And, unfortunately, there wasn't even anything under the beds. So all we can do is have a tod for the bod and make the best of being alone."

Moira had used to shock a lot of people, including Howard. But she had never shocked Sara. It was odd. Many of the things she said should have shocked her. If someone else had said them they would have. But Moira had always occupied a special place in her life, giving her a taste, perhaps, of what she might have been if she had just been otherwise. Moira had been a career girl, the real thing, and therefore, in Sara's mind at least, exempt from the normal restrictions of the female mystique.

Thinking of Moira made Sara feel better. She let go of her wrist with a faint smile and stood up. The radio announcer was giving the weather. There was no rain in sight in Texas either. Sara gave a long sigh that filled her lungs and restored her self-respect. She took off her robe and got into her gown. Then she went into the living room and looked at the intercom box. All I have to do, she thought, is punch a button and that nice Mr. Bishop will answer me. There will be a voice, and then a presence coming right up in the elevator if I need him. I simply can't feel morbid because I'm alone. I'm going to be alone from now on.

There were still two packing cases in the middle of the living room. One of them contained Howard's books and records and personal things. The other, miscellaneous junk they hadn't been able to part with. She saw that it was still only a few minutes after ten and that she could unpack those two boxes, but on second thought she decided to save them for tomorrow night.

Tomorrow night, she thought, and her mind skittered away. She picked up the magazine she'd brought with her and slid into her newly made bed. She flipped through the magazine casually, looking at all the ads for all the beautiful things for all the beautiful people.

She wasn't one of the beautiful people; but she had managed, because of Howard, of course, to have most of the beautiful things. As she had on other occasions of loneliness she listed them in her mind, trying to recall the joy they had brought at the time of acquiring, the feeling of safety and solidity they had always given her. She thought of her home in Minneapolis with each of its appliances in its appointed place, each piece of furniture placed carefully on the carpet. She hung each dress on its hanger in the closet and remembered with love the Christmas of the pearls, the sapphire, the ruby bracelet.

She woke with a start to find the bed lamp shining in her eyes. But she still felt comforted and sleepy and switched it off, falling into sleep without noticing the gap she'd left where the fur coat had arrived. Her mind gave her instead her crystal mouse and she drifted soundly into sleep thinking of his crystal tail.

Something woke her suddenly and she jerked awake, realizing in the moment of waking it had been the magazine sliding off the bed onto the floor. She looked at her watch. The hands pointed to two-thirty. She felt abused, as though she must have slept longer than that and that it wasn't fair of her watch to remind her that time was still running far too slow even as she slept.

Two-thirty was not a good time to waken in the night. It was still far too early to think about dawn, seconds and minutes and hours of time away. She had read somewhere once that most of the crimes committed in the country were committed between the hours of eleven and two. But at this moment that didn't make her feel better. It was not really time to relax yet. Only at three-thirty, which was very close to four and daylight, could one feel lulled into sleeping. Two-thirty was still the middle of the night.

She lay rigid in her narrow twin bed and listened to the darkness around her. Then she had a good thought in her wakefulness. The other occupants of the building must have come home by now. She thought of them, sleeping restlessly or soundly, snoring, mumbling nonsense in their beds around her. Some of them would be getting up to flush the johns, sending water through the miles of condominium pipes; some of them, perhaps, going to the refrigerator for late-early snacks; some of them, even, making love. There might be children here—though she doubted it. One might wake and call for something in the night, as Howie used to do, saying Wa-wa, Ma, saying all the half-asleep cozy things babies said. Standing, eyes still half shut in cuddly feeted pajamas, holding onto the edge of a crib, with the creases from sleeping on the blanket in his cheeks. When she had held Howie he had always been warm, almost hot, to the touch, a small furnace warming up her nights.

Howie was a grown man in New Zealand with a pretty little wife with long hair and bare feet and a mind of her own. Sara liked his pretty little hippie wife, but she'd never been able to tell her so. She supposed the sloppiness had put her off. But there was something of Moira in Howie's Ely. And something of herself. Though Ely was small and quick and dark, neither self-possessed like Moira nor slow in little ways like Sara herself.

"Is her name really Ely?" she had said to Howie.

He'd looked at her with that raised-eyebrow, oh-come-on-now-Ma look, and said, "Yes, Mother. Ely. I think it's rather nice, don't you?"

"I think it's different," Sara had said.

She thought about them, with their baby, living Down Under in a world she couldn't imagine. Then she put the thought away.

She could see the hall light raying into her room across the expanse of carpet. She wondered what she'd done with her package of cigarettes. She remembered the days when she'd been a smoker and always had them handy on the bedside table and she felt put-upon that they weren't there now.

She got up reluctantly and padded into the dark kitchen. The cigarettes were lying on the edge of the sink and she took the pack and lit one. She wandered through the apartment, dragging on the cigarette, coming finally to the balcony doors. She opened them and went out into the night. It was warmer outside and just a trifle muggy, but there was a breeze from the Gulf that whipped her nightgown around her bare legs and that contained still, even in April, a hint of northern chill.

She looked out and down. The scene hadn't changed. There was still the empty lighted pool, the dark empty Gulf, the dark and empty building around her. She looked toward her neigh-

31

bor's balcony. No light. She listened into the night. Only a faint soughing from the Gulf.

She finished her cigarette and put it out carefully in the shell on her wrought-iron porch table. She turned toward her balcony doors, gripped suddenly by the fear she'd shut them behind her and was locked onto the balcony. It would be so typical of her, Howard would say, and so ridiculous. There would be no way in at all. She didn't even have her high-heeled mules with which to break the glass.

Of course, she hadn't closed the door at all. When she faced it there was the faint line of space showing emptily between the sheets of polished glass. Through the glass she could see her crystal shining in the hallway light, reflecting itself back and forth from figure to figure, filling the shelves with a satisfying bulk, making this place hers.

Standing there, looking in, she imagined herself walking across the living room and herself—or perhaps some other?—watching her from the balcony. She didn't like the image and quickly slid the doors open, slipping through and locking them behind her.

She stood there, just inside the door, and began to cry. Because she knew, quite simply, and in spite of the fact that her mind was telling her that it was stupid, that she was going to have to search the apartment again.

I just won't do it, she told herself. I'll calmly go back to bed. But she knew she would, and she did, though this time the search was cursory. Still, she made it, compulsively and with pounding heart.

She went back to bed, but this time she didn't try to sleep. She put her cigarettes on the bedside table, switched on the bed lamp, and picked up her magazine.

She had always hated the times when Howard had had to be out of town on business, always been nervous and frightened in the house alone. She used to bring Howie into the room with her so that if they had to flee she would have him close. Over the years she'd developed elaborate schemes of escape, but none of those plans had ever kept her from making that silly search through the nighttime house.

"It's all nonsense," Howard would say. "You don't really expect to find anything, of course. For God sakes, what would you do if you did? You know damned well you don't expect someone to be standing in one of those closets when you throw open the door. If you did you'd never have the nerve to open it."

True, of course, but irrelevant to the compulsion.

Sara's eyes refocused on the paragraph she had read three times without making any sense of it. She had come now to the crux of the matter. She was behaving in exactly the way Howard would have expected her to behave. She wasn't coping.

Howard had always been convinced that she *couldn't* cope. She sometimes thought he'd based their whole marriage on that simple fact: that poor Sara didn't and couldn't exist without him, that she was incapable of decision, action, simple being, without him to direct her in it.

How, she often thought, does he think I managed to survive in the years before I met him? Of course, there had been very few of those years and most of them had been spent under the protection of her family.

Still, she thought, why is it nothing I ever did seemed to count for anything? I raised Howie, and I did all right, I guess. He never liked me very much, I don't think. But then, he didn't like Howard very much either. And he is coping with his world, he and Ely. They seem to be coping very well.

Howard never did any of those dull rotten things for Howie either. Changing diapers, and taking him to the park, and driving him to nursery school, and standing at the bus corner. *I* did all that. And *I* coped very well.

I did all the things about the house too. I furnished it and kept it. And I entertained. I learned to drive too, even though I hated it. And I've made myself fly on airplanes and put other people on them all these years. And it wasn't ever easy, no matter what Howard thought.

She put the magazine down on the bed. She sat still against her pillows, very conscious of herself, enclosed in her own skin, a living being in a world of living beings, alone and talking still to Howard, who simply was not there any more.

But it was as some sort of challenge to Howard that she made herself still her heart, which was pounding away too loudly in the night, that she made herself get up and make coffee and drink a cup, that she read carefully a rather dull story about yet another housewife too confined.

When she finished the story it was four o'clock. Outside the Florida night was still dark, but Sara knew that the dawn was just moments away. She knew that no one, not even one of those strange children she feared and wished she didn't fear would be apt to be involved in breaking and entering at this hour so close to daylight, knew that soon there would be newspaper boys throwing rolled papers against porches, milkmen whistling through the dawn with clinking bottles and snarls at barking dogs, fishermen rising early and stowing gear into cars, early travelers rising to catch the six-o'clock plane to Atlanta.

Her four-o'clock bed was warm and cozy. She snuggled under the covers, threw the extra pillow onto the floor, and sank gratefully into sleep.

But her dreams betrayed her, even as dawn came, not out of the Gulf, as she always mistakenly imagined it, nor like thunder, as her mind still attuned to high-school Kipling thought of it, but quietly and gently from the landside to the east. Her dreams threw up endless corridors with blank gray walls and miles of neutral gray carpet, lined with closed doors behind which empty space beguiled the unwary and through which—the doors once opened—she would fall forever, stopped only, if at all, by a grasping hand, one that wasn't friendly, and that she had just as soon not have been grasped by at all.

In sleep, Sara Hillstrom tossed and moaned softly, not coping, just as Howard would have said.

Chapter 3

The sun woke her. It streamed into the apartment through the uncurtained windows, dazzling in its early morning brilliance, touching her face with the joy of suns of childhood, holding promise and excitement, and the eternal recurring miracle of Again.

Sara sat up, stretched, yawned, smiled. She had the exact feeling she'd had on Saturday mornings during school days, knowing there was a new full day ahead with nothing onerous to spoil it.

With full awakening she realized her error, but her joy wasn't dampened. She was shocked at the joy and for a moment she groped for images of sadness to exculpate herself. Then she gave it up and got out of bed and made her coffee. I'm going to treat myself to breakfast out, she thought. I can do that.

She had always loved to eat breakfast out. It gave her a marvelous feeling compounded in equal parts of luxury and licentiousness, as though she were very rich and pampered for being able to afford to do it, and as though she had come from some exciting and sinful romping of the night before straight to a staid restaurant with the mark of it still on her. She had never in her life come from such a romping to a public breakfast. In fact, she mocked herself in the sunlight, she'd never even had such a sinful romping. But the fact of it always sat with her at breakfast out. Just as the fact of luxury sat with the two-dollar eggs.

I'm becoming a ridiculous old woman, she told herself. But she had always felt this way. She had just never told anyone. Howard would have snorted. Moira would have looked worried. Anyone else she knew would have been patronizingly amused. The fact was, she was amused herself. She hummed as she washed her coffee cup and went to take a shower.

How different the bathroom seemed in this morning sunshine; blue and white and shining. The water from the shower sparkled onto the tiles. When she got out she rubbed the steam from the mirror with her hand and looked at her face as though it belonged to a friendly person.

She toweled herself dry and then remembered that she'd stuffed the clothes of yesterday into the hamper. She got into her robe and went to see what she'd brought over from the other place. Nothing really, she thought, gazing into the half-empty closet. They'd started moving clothes, but had only brought the things they didn't wear very often. Hanging beside a sober suit of Howard's and a very loud suit of Howard's—that even he had admitted was a mistake—were only the clothes she wore on odd occasions: the cocktail dresses and the suits she thought of as "my Minneapolis suits," far too heavy for Florida. There was also a yellow dress she felt made her look sallow and an orange dress that she'd bought for Florida and never had the nerve to wear. Well, I'll have to wear it, she thought, and put it on before she could change her mind.

The whole apartment seemed to have subtly changed. Shape, size, color. The gray of the rugs seemed exactly right for the Florida sun, the lightness of the walls perfectly attuned to the stripes of sunlight coming into the rooms. On her shelves her crystal gleamed, glittered, glistened. She crossed to it and put her hand gently on her crystal mouse.

Before going out she went out on her balcony and looked at the Gulf. The tide was in this morning and the waves rolled majestically onto the beach. She glanced quickly at the balcony across the way, but there was no one there. There weren't even any chairs on it, she noticed. Perhaps they don't like feeling crowded, she thought. I think mine is a little crowded. She frowned at her iron furniture, shrugged and went inside. She hesitated, looking at the door, then locked it, feeling it was a sensible habit. She got her purse and went into the corridor.

Surprisingly, it looked no different with daylight. It was still a long muted hallway of soft light and closed doors. She walked down it in silence and entered the soundless elevator.

In the parking area she stood still for a moment, puzzled. Across the way she could see her car, sitting in front of 12 B just as she had left it last night. But it was now, as it had been then, the only car visible. She looked at her watch. It was eight-thirty. Surely the inhabitants of the Triton didn't have to be at work.

Sunlight fell through the slots in the sides of the garage in patches, losing its beach brilliance in the subterranean gloom. A feeling of foreboding nibbled at the edges of her morning mood, but she pushed it away. Nonetheless, she looked into the back seat, just as though it were night, before getting into the car.

The winding way out of the garage seemed shorter going out than it had coming in, perhaps because there was the square of light beckoning from the bottom of the last turn. She exited into sunlight and braked the car, fumbling in her purse for her sunglasses. The new green of the tended lawn, glimpsed through their grayness, seemed artificial, the round globes of the extinguished lights part of a stage set. There was no one in sight, not even Mr. Bishop. Though, of course, she told herself, he must have been relieved. But where then was the day man?

As though summoned up by the magic of her thought, a young man came around the side of the building. He looked startled at the sight of her. He was wearing white slacks and a blue-and-white striped shirt and sneakers. He walked toward her car, frowning.

"Who are you?" he said when he reached the window.

"Why, I'm Mrs. Hillstrom in 12 B," she said, and wondered instantly why she hadn't said, "Who are *you?*"

"You mean you're living here?" he said.

"Yes," she said. "May I ask who you are?"

The young man smiled. "Sorry," he said. "You startled me. I didn't know any . . . you'd moved in. I'm Theo Snyder, the builder's representative. I don't believe I sold to you."

"No," she said. "You didn't. My husband bought our apartment before the building was even started."

"Ah," he said. "And when did you move in?"

There was something about his manner that put Sara off. She felt as though he were quizzing her about some strange action on her part and that, on the contrary, she should have been quizzing him. "We began moving in a week or so ago," she said. And she thought, Why did I say *we?*

"Then you spent the night here?" he said.

"Yes, Mr. Snyder," she said.

"Well . . . glad to have you," he said, backing away from the car now. "I have a temporary office just inside. Should you hear of anyone else interested in one of our condominiums . . . some friends perhaps . . ." The smile enlarged, seemed artificial.

"I need my breakfast, Mr. Snyder," Sara said hastily. "Good morning."

She drove away quickly, leaving him standing at the entrance of the building looking after her.

He was not at all, she thought as she turned onto the highway, like the night watchman, Mr. Bishop. There was nothing reassuring in his manner. In fact, he reminded her of the scuffling teenagers she'd seen at the phone booth last night. She didn't know why. He was clean-shaven, his hair, though longer than anyone's used to be, wasn't really long. Still, there was a certain looseness in his stance, a mocking quality in his smile. He didn't seem at all the sort of young man who should have been a builder's representative.

Howie would have laughed at her. "Christ, Ma," he'd have said. "The world keeps right on moving. It happens. It's no more or less frightening than it ever was."

But it is, Howie, she thought. Maybe not for you. But for me.

Howard would have said, "Impudent rascal." And that would have been the end of that.

She was aware that the pristine emotion with which she had greeted the day was evaporating rapidly as she drove toward the shopping circle and she strove to recapture it, thinking of the comfort of the restaurant and the enjoyment of breakfast ahead of her.

The place she chose was as bright and cheerful as she could have wished it. It was a chain restaurant, new and clean and sparkling. The waitresses were local girls wearing the standard uniform of the chain, but sporting the tan and bleached hair that made them Florida's own. She sat in a booth, which she always preferred to a table, and sniffed at the good smells in the air. One of the pretty girls brought water and filled her coffee cup. She wanted fried eggs, but prudence and habit made her order soft-boiled. She did make her own small gesture toward sin by having scrapple.

While she waited, she sipped her coffee and looked at the other customers. There were several families who seemed to be tourists, wearing beach clothes and looking abnormally pink, as though they'd stayed too long in the sun yesterday. One small boy stood precariously on the edge of his chair, causing his mother to make ineffectual and irritated grabs at him until his father finally settled the matter with a grim swat to his backside.

Several businessmen in sober suits sat together in a corner discussing papers they'd pulled from their brief cases. They looked hurried and harried already so early in the day. They try too hard, Sara thought. That was always the trouble with Howard. Everything, even the games, has to be of primal importance to men.

She felt that she'd had a very good thought and she wished she knew how to pursue it. She had never had the least belief in her own intelligence and any abstract thought that came to her always made her feel as though it were someone else's, transported suddenly and strangely, by some form of ESP, into her head.

In the booth next to her a young couple sat side by side. They looked happy and involved with each other, oblivious to the day, the restaurant, the people around them. Occasionally the girl would reach over shyly and put her hand on the young man's arm. She caught Sara watching her and blushed. Sara smiled and the girl smiled back.

Somewhere behind her two people were having a quarrel. The voices were low and the words indistinguishable, but the tone was unmistakable. There would be the male voice: firm, serious, explanatory—furious. Then the female: nervous, ragged, defensive—sad. Then a silence, and the same thing all over again.

Sara's breakfast came and she stared at her two boiled eggs in the thick white cup. That is never going to happen to me again, she thought. I am never going to be lectured to with my breakfast. The thought was, oddly, one of sadness.

Moira had always said she wouldn't put up with that no matter what. She was herself, her own person, and no one, certainly no man, would ever tell her how to live and what to do. She said it simply wasn't worth it. You paid for freedom from loneliness by losing your self-respect. Self-respect, she said, won hands down with her. Loneliness she could live with. But if you've never had its opposite how can you really know loneliness? Sara thought. And while her mind grappled with that new and disturbing thought, she ate her eggs.

Only after she had finished her breakfast did she think of the morning paper. She wasn't in the habit of reading the paper with breakfast because Howard always did that. He liked a fresh new paper and it didn't matter to her. She read it during the afternoon. She got up and went to the counter and bought one to read with her third cup of coffee.

She wondered if all this coffee was going to make her nervous. But it never had. That was only something people said, she was sure. Eating oatmeal made her nervous and it certainly didn't other people. From this she deduced it was all just something in people's minds.

She didn't let the newspaper make her nervous either. That, of course, could make anyone nervous. But you had to read it with a certain detachment. It certainly wouldn't do to read the front page news and *feel* all of it. Nor the local news either, for that matter. Today there was the usual casualty report from the East, and the usual Washington report which would mean more money out of her pocket eventually, and the usual local-government report which was just plain boondoggling. She turned to the editorial page and read William Buckley, even though he often baffled her, and Art Buchwald, even though he always did.

Then she turned to the local news and read about the accidents on the Tamiami Trail and the arrests for possession of marijuana. She read the local-gossip reporter because there was usually something about someone she knew slightly and she read Earl Wilson because everyone knew all those people slightly. She read the obituary column because she always did.

The funnies didn't really interest her, but she read them faithfully, always hoping, perhaps, that they would. Moira had been a great admirer of Pogo. Howie had liked him too, and Peanuts. Howard liked Li'l Abner. She had never found any of them very funny, but she did smile at Andy Capp; and she had to admit to a weakness for Poteet Canyon. The rest of them she read from habit, even Little Orphan Annie, which had been boring her to death all her life.

The other customers were leaving the restaurant and she knew she should get up and go, but she wasn't sure yet what she was going to do with her day. It had seemed so full of possibilities when she'd wakened into it and so bereft of them at this moment. That young man at the Triton and the newspaper seemed to have taken something out of it. She got up though, paid her check, and went outside to her car briskly, just as though there were many things needing her attention and many people waiting for her call. The little shopping circle looked elegant and busy, but she was in no mood for shopping. She sat in the car for a few moments, then turned on the motor and drove toward the old apartment to finish packing her things.

She tried to keep her mind on the mechanics of driving, because she knew quite well she didn't dare look at the enormous emptiness of this new day. It was a sudden and simple fact that once looked at could not be looked away from. There had to be something; something waiting somewhere in the next moment, day, week. Otherwise no one would go on with the ridiculously dull things like eating and drinking and reading Little Orphan Annie, and driving an automobile from one place to another. One simply couldn't look at a future, at even a day, containing nothing but those mechanics of life. How could any human being, even Sara Hillstrom have arrived at the brink of that enormous emptiness? How could anyone live fifty years and not have anything waiting for that next moment, week, month?

You could not blame it on marriage and death. It could not be just that Howard had been the only thing and he was gone. If she had been the one to die Howard would still have had some sort of life. He could have looked forward to the golf course or the poker table, even to Minneapolis. Maybe it wouldn't have been fun for him, not for a while. But he would have been able to fill a day. It wasn't just her sex either. She had known other women whose husbands had died. They were miserable. But they kept living. There was something that they could have been thinking of doing to fill the next moment. They didn't stop. And looking straight at that enormous emptiness could only lead to that. A full stop.

She had felt the day full of possibilities this morning. The sunlight had seemed full of possibilities. What had she thought of then? Of a time when just sunlight was enough? The promise of a day without school to be filled with anything at all? But those were the thoughts of youth. And when you are young anything is possible. The future contains the universe. She had used up all the possibilities. She had married and had a son and run a house. The husband and son and house were gone. There were still the things to finish packing in the old apartment. Her mind clutched at the simple fact. There was, after all, something for the next moment. There was that to keep the specter of emptiness away.

There were shadows on the shallow front porch and she put the key in the lock with a comfortable feeling of familiarity and went into the dark living room. Already the place smelled faintly musty as though no one lived there any more. And, of course, no one did.

She went to her little desk and made a purposeful list of all the things she had to do: the TV people and the telephone people and the paper. She dialed the cable people and they told her she'd have to move the set herself. They'd be happy to hook her in on the apartment cable, no charge, but not until tomorrow. She called the paper and they agreed to change her address, but said it would probably take several days. She called the phone company and after speaking to three different girls and being given a sales pitch on colored princess phones by all three she finally got someone to promise to have this one disconnected, "sometime this week," and her new one in, "sometime this week."

"But I need it," she said.

This time she was given a speech about all the people who left town without paying their bills.

She hung up finally, feeling frustrated and on the verge of tears. Everything seemed to be proving so difficult. What was the matter with her? First she wanted things to do, then she resented the very things that were coming her way. She looked balefully at the television set, and called the moving men. They told her that just by luck they had a load out to her key tomorrow and they could take her things along. She felt as though she had been given a gift.

There was very little left in the apartment to pack; she got it all into two big boxes, and pushed and pulled them into the room beside the television set. Then she allowed herself to look at her watch. It was almost noon. She could think about lunch.

She locked the apartment and went around the end of the unit to the door of the manager's apartment and knocked. He came to the door, a paper napkin in his hand, and began commiserating with her again, using all the words he'd used before, the first day, and at the funeral. She listened politely, nodding, and then told him the movers would be there tomorrow for the last of her things. She gave him the key from her key ring, got in her car, and drove away from that part of her life.

She decided to have lunch at the marina restaurant. It was a bright and happy place in the noontime, and though she'd been glad she hadn't gone the night before, she was pleased to be able to turn in there now. The restaurant was on the second floor, a glass-walled eyrie, from which there was a marvelous view of the bay and harbor. Some people said it was much too glary in the daytime, but Sara welcomed the glare, though she had to keep her sunglasses on. She was shown to a corner table from which she had a view of all the boats in the harbor.

Sara had always loved the idea of boats. It had been one of the romantic corners of her soul, the dream of relaxing aboard with a salt spray coming over the rail and the waves against the hull. She knew now that boats weren't like that at all. She knew that they were frightening, and recalcitrant, and dangerous. Because Howard had bought one. It was a trim, expensive cruiser with dazzling white paint and a powerful motor and a wide deck on which to relax in that salt spray of dream. Sara had outfitted them both in yachting clothes, had stocked the galley with both practical and exotic things, feeling a fulfillment hitherto unknown to her. She had gone on board for the maiden voyage, expecting the experience of a lifetime. And she had been frightened out of her mind. She had never had one peaceful moment on that boat. She had been afraid it would turn over, would catch on fire, would sink unreasonably and completely and cast her into the immensity of the Gulf of Mexico.

Her reaction to the *Pelican* had angered Howard more than anything she had ever done in their married life. He had berated her and scoffed at her and yelled at her. Finally, he had sold the boat. "It's no damned fun with someone having the screaming meemies on the fantail," he'd said.

Now, looking at the boats in the harbor with their owners peacefully, even happily, getting ready to cast off, she had another of the alien thoughts that had been plaguing her today. *Howard was afraid of that boat too,* the informer in her head said. *He didn't really like it any better than you did.*

She was embarrassed, and she looked around quickly as though someone might have heard the thought. No one was looking her way, not even the waiter. But then, waiters never looked her way.

Eventually one paused at her table by pure accident and asked her if she'd like a drink before lunch. The request always embarrassed her. She felt that she should want a drink, should have one just to accommodate the waiter who no doubt needed the time she would consume by having it. When Howard was with her it didn't matter, because, of course, he would have one, leaving her free to decline if she so desired. Now, alone, she hesitated. "Why yes," she said, finally, reluctantly. "Perhaps so."

The waiter, a young man with long sideburns, waited impatiently, slouched on one foot. Her mind rejected Howard's bourbon, Moira's martini, various concoctions of friends. Then she remembered an advertisement seen in a magazine, a lovely, sophisticated woman reclining like a cat on a brocaded sofa, a sparkling glass held in elegant hands.

"A Bacardi?" she said.

He went away with no indication of surprise, so she presumed she'd said it right, and soon the glass arrived, looking just as it had in the advertisement. She smiled her thanks and sipped at it tentatively. It tasted rather nasty, she thought, but interesting. She must keep her mind on how interesting everything could be.

She sipped doggedly at the drink and gazed at the beautiful boats, and oddly enough she began to feel rather nice, cozy, almost as though she were that woman on the sofa, a giant cat, satisfied and full of canary.

She quickly sat upright. This is why people drink, she thought. And I do not really like it. She raised her hand imperiously and the waiter miraculously appeared and took her order for the seaboat salad. She looked distrustfully at the rest of the Bacardi and pushed it away, thinking of poor Mimi Stanton.

Mimi had been the prettiest and brightest girl in the Minneapolis of the generation before Sara's. She was a sort of Midwestern Zelda Fitzgerald, only rich in her own right, because her father had invented some marvelous substance to make women beautiful and had known enough—so Howard always said—to convince them of it. She had shone at the country club dances and horse shows and symphony openings, and hardly anyone—certainly not Sara Hillstrom—had known there was any misery or desperation in her life when the fact had been circulated that she'd died in the alcoholic ward of a private hospital.

Sara had heard a lot more about it afterward because Moira had almost married her son, only that stern strict thing in Moira that said, No man will tell me how to live, had meant it, even though the price had been several million dollars. And Moira had probably been right, because the son was dead now too. And had been for twenty years.

Of course, Sara's still Bacardi-struck mind said, Moira's dead too. And Howard. But then we . . . they . . . didn't die twenty years ago.

She ate her seaboat salad and thought about the strangeness of the fact of twenty years. It should have been a long time. It was almost a quarter of a century. But it wasn't really any time. It disappeared and who knew where it had gone. Only those mute reminders on her shelves. The crystal pieces crying, I am 1955. I am 1963.

"Why, Sara Hillstrom," a voice said behind her. She jumped, almost knocking her water glass over, and turned, tentatively, to see a woman who, for the moment, she didn't recognize at all.

"Sara?" the woman, tall, emaciated, and tiredly elegant, said. "Don't you remember me?"

Sara's mind dropped back the requisite twenty years she'd just been contemplating and thought, Mary Appleby? Surely not. Yes it is. "Why, hello, Mary," she said.

The tall figure moved around the table and gestured at a chair and Sara said, "Yes. Sit down. Do. What are you doing in Cape Haze?"

Mary, eyes darting around the room and zeroing in on the waiter in perfect synchronization, said, "Let me order us an after-luncheon drink. What're you having?" And to the quickly appearing waiter, "Another of the same for both of us." And to Sara, "For God sakes, darling, tell me all about what you've been doing with yourself."

The words brought a grotesque picture to Sara's mind. A scene of secret darkened self-gratification, practiced desperately in fear and guilt in an empty twin bed.

"Doing with myself?" she said inanely. "Why, nothing, of course."

"Oh Sara," Mary said. "You haven't changed at all. You never will. It cheers me up, dear. It really does. You don't even *look* different. It's marvelous. You must have come to Florida and actually discovered good old Ponce de You-know-who's fountain of you-know-what."

Sara smiled. Then wondered why she had, because, of course, the first thing she was going to have to do was tell Mary about Howard.

The drinks came and Mary raised a martini on the rocks at her. Sara raised a new Bacardi at her and blurted out, "Howard died this week."

Mary had a little trouble negotiating the gulp of martini she was taking, put the glass down, and said, "Oh dear."

"I'm sorry," Sara said.

Mary raised plucked eyebrows. *"You're* sorry?" she said. "My God, Sara. *I'm* sorry. That's the way it should go."

"Well, I blurted it out like that," Sara said. "I . . . you know . . . didn't want you asking about him."

"We're getting to that age, aren't we?" Mary said sadly. Sara noticed she'd recovered her aplomb. "You never dare ask any more. You really don't. If it isn't death, it's likely to be divorce or dissolution."

"How have you been, Mary?" Sara said.

"I'm fine, darling," Mary said. "I'm always fine. You know that. I'm between husbands now. I'd say through with husbands, but you'd know I didn't mean it. I never have. I never will. I just like men around. God knows why."

Yes, Sara thought. You always did. All the way back through those fast-going years to high school.

"They like you too," she said.

"Not really," Mary said. "My God. I could never have had one around forever the way you did Howard." She finished her drink and looked at Sara's still-full glass. "You still don't drink, I see," she said. "What are you doing, dear? Where do you live?"

Sara was relieved to have a definite something to talk about. Mary Appleby, as always, made her feel self-conscious, naïve, and just a wee bit dumb.

"We'd just bought a new condominium," she said. "I moved in last night. It's going to be very nice . . . once I get used to it."

"Which one, dear?" Mary said, signaling the waiter again. "I live in one too, you know—a rented one—so I don't even have to think about it."

"The Triton," Sara said. "On Pirate Key." She felt, for the first time, a certain pride in her address. It was a good building, a new one, an expensive one.

"The Triton?" Mary said, and the eyebrows raised again in puzzlement. "But it isn't open yet."

"Oh yes it is," Sara said. "I live there."

"But how strange," Mary said. "I have a friend who owns one of the apartments there, and she went off to Europe just a week ago because she said nobody had moved in and she wasn't about to until she had some company."

The feeling of uneasiness in Sara's stomach turned into a small tight knot. She picked up the new Bacardi. "I'm there," she said.

Mary shrugged. "Oh well," she said brightly. "That was a week ago. I suppose people have moved in in the meantime."

I want to cry, Sara thought. But I won't. "It's really a beautiful place," she said.

"I know," Mary said. "It's better than mine. But I simply couldn't bear the bother of *owning* anything. Cecil—my last—wanted to buy me one, but I said, 'No, precious, just sign this little thingy that says you're liable for the rent forever and I'll take that.' They *do* more for you when you have no responsibility yourself. That, I fear, is the way of our evil world. But then . . ." She drank deeply and giggled. "You never have thought of our world as evil, have you, Sara?"

Why does she keep saying things like that to me? Sara thought. She's making fun of me in some silly way, just as she used to in high school, and, just as then, I don't know whether it's mean of her or not. I truly don't know whether she wants to hurt me or whether there's something about me she just can't resist picking at. She listened to hear if the alien voice was going to give her a thought she could use about Mary. But it didn't.

Mary's face was undergoing a subtle transformation as she tucked into the new drink. Finally she reached a hand across the table and patted Sara's arm. "Sara, dammit," she said, and for a moment her voice carried a reality and conviction Sara had never heard in it before. "I *am* sorry about Howard. I just simply can't *say* things like that."

"I know," Sara said.

She thought, Well, I do know. And somehow that is rather awful, and I wish I didn't. I really wish I was exactly the way Mary thinks I am. That the possibility of evil just didn't exist for me.

"I want to buy you another drink," Mary said.

"No thanks, Mary," Sara said. "I've hardly touched this one. Honestly."

An ugly look crossed the well-groomed face. "Do you think I'm drinking too much?" Mary said. "That would be just like you, Sara. You always used to sit around with that holier-than-thou expression. Even when we were kids. Good God, it even used to bother you if somebody skipped school and went to the lake for the afternoon."

Sara wondered what Mary would say if she told her that it really hadn't bothered her at all in the sense Mary meant. That she'd only wished somebody had wanted her to lay out and go to the lake with them. But she supposed Mary wouldn't believe her if she said so. Or she would laugh. Or she'd just get up and go.

Sara realized she didn't want Mary to get up and go. Even though she'd never really liked her, could see no possibility of future friendship developing from this chance encounter, still, she didn't want her to leave. She was a voice, a human presence in the afternoon sunlight, and when she left silence would come back. The afternoon would stretch long toward evening. And evening would bring . . . two boxes to unpack in a silent, empty . . .

"Mary," she said, in a voice she hoped was bright, "I will have another Bacardi after all."

"Well, goody," Mary said. "Only, why do you drink that stuff? Do you really like it? Wouldn't you rather have a good knock of Scotch?" She smiled, the mean look coming back. "I wouldn't dare suggest a martini, of course."

Sara hastily drank from her almost-full glass. "This is fine, for now," she said.

"O.K.," Mary said, looking at her diamond-studded watch. "After all it's only two. Three more hours before a decent sun goes over a decent yardarm."

She signaled the waiter again, and looking at her face, Sara realized the voice was going to speak to her after all. She was beginning to welcome it, as well as be somewhat shocked by it. This time it said quite clearly, Mary has exactly the same expression on her face Howard used to get after he'd had half-a-dozen bourbons.

It made her look at Mary with interest. It gave her a gauge and a way to deal with her. She calmly let the waiter carry off her two half-full glasses, and took the new one with every sign of enjoyment.

"You know, Mary," she said shyly, not quite realizing the artifice with which she could bring forth that shyness, "you really look just fabulous. As you always did. I can hardly believe it's been . . . well . . ." She laughed deprecatingly . . . "All those years since we sat in old Mr. Riemer's math class."

"God, don't mention that old queen," Mary said. But Sara could see that her good humor had been restored.

"I thought for sure he'd flunk me senior year," she went on. "And, my God, what would I have done? After all, I'd failed at that fancy school they'd tried to keep me in. If I hadn't been able to pass at home I'd never have gotten to college and Otis Brent."

Otis had been Mary's first husband, Sara remembered. And he'd been rich, as had been two others of her subsequent three. The only one who hadn't been had looked like Paul Newman.

Sara had let her guard down. She was feeling, and this time it had nothing to do with the half-sipped Bacardis, rather like the smug lady on the brocaded sofa in the magazine. She was actually handling Mary Appleby, that feared and admired girl of her youth, who always knew the right thing to say, whose skirts always hung beautifully, whose remarks always made the boys laugh.

"It was fun, in the old days—Minneapolis," she said.

There must have been a betraying wistfulness in her voice, or a sound of insincerity. Mary put down her glass and looked at her with eyes grown a little hard.

"I never thought you liked it," she said.

Sara saved herself. "Well, I was always shy," she said.

That pleased. But maybe not enough. Mary looked restless. Her beautifully coiffed and dyed head turned to look around the bright room, returned reluctantly to Sara. Her eyes narrowed. She smiled, that ancient smile of superiority and brutality.

"Well, you always had Moira to speak up for you," she said.

The words brought a terrible pang to Sara's heart. Much more so than telling Mary about Howard had done. She thought of all the girl talk and all the confidences, all the acceptances Moira had given her when nobody else would.

"Moira's dead too now," she said.

Out in the bay the boats seemed to rock in a sudden fall of shadow. She could see the lines attaching them unstably to land, smell, in memory, the gasoline, that flammable substance which Howard scoffed at her for believing flammable. A man stood on the deck of one nearest the window and he seemed a threatening figure. He looked like the young man, Theo Snyder, who had come to her car this morning at the condominium. He threw a lighted cigarette into the water and she half expected to see the oil-slick waters explode into flame, spreading fire to the whole marina, sending spreading tendrils of flame toward the peaceful, now almost-empty restaurant.

"I didn't know that," Mary said.

Sara stood up, looking at Mary in a clear hard bright seeing. Mary was a drunken old woman, wasting away the daytime drinking martinis, bringing to a casual luncheon table old thoughts, reactions, memories, of two long-dead girls. Sara and Mary no longer existed as high school cohorts. They no longer lived in the land of the lakes in the innocence of life not yet begun. They were two old women at a lonely table in too much sunlight. And Mary probably wasn't any good at boats either.

"I have to go," Sara said. "I have an appointment."

Mary looked up at her, startled. "Well, call me, Sara," she said. "I'm at the Twin Towers on Sombre Key. Call me." She laughed. "The name's Carrol. Mary Carrol."

"Yes," Sara said. "I will, Mary. Thanks for the drinks."

Sara felt tears close again and knew they were because she was thinking, But you're no good to me. You're no good at all.

She turned and went quickly down the stairs and into the afternoon sunlight. She drove out of the marina quickly and was over the bridge and on the way back to the condominium without conscious thought. She didn't even stop in the shopping circle, forgetting her desire to buy groceries in the gourmet food store. She was on her way home. Home, the place to escape Mary Appleby and her superior smile, the place to escape the marina and the boats that proved to be not beautiful and free, but dangerous and binding, the place to escape the fact that no one saved you. Nothing did.

But from what did she want to be saved? The question came unbidden into her mind as she fled toward the condominium, hated last night, needed now. Not from boats and dangerous living. She *had* saved herself from that. Always. She had even, by her refusal to go back to Minneapolis, saved herself from having to consider getting a job there, taking work from well-meaning acquaintances of Howard's—something to do with her days. She had just, at this very hour, saved herself from Mary Appleby and her social life. The same Mary Appleby and the same, in essence, social life she had saved herself from years ago. You did all the things; you saved yourself. And in the end you could say, Nothing saves you. Because she might not have to do a single thing she didn't want to, nor feel a single thing she wasn't capable of feeling; but the very absence of those things and feelings was what was driving her now. And driving her toward the thing she didn't want to look at, the emptiness of that apartment in an empty life. Well, it was what she had. There was still somewhere to go. She was on the way home.

But as she rounded the turn by the golf course and saw the

bulking tower of concrete ahead of her she knew that even the word home had no meaning any more. From somewhere, possibly the depths of high school remembrances that Mary Appleby had stirred within her, possibly from the sweetish fumes of Bacardi in the sunlight, an old sentence of portending disastrous fate came back to her. It ran through her mind like a frightened mouse in a maze, like her crystal mouse come real into a world unreal in its reality. The sentence was: *Childe Roland to the Dark Tower Came.*

Chapter 4

The building loomed ahead of her, clean-lined, modern, an efficient edifice in the efficient world of the 1970s. It didn't appear so to her. It was a castle, seen often on the covers of paperback books, and always with a running girl in the foreground. Even the ocean didn't seem to her a southern, sand-edged ocean; rather a dark northern ocean with cliffs and caves and caverns. An ocean for Annabel Lee, or Jane Eyre, or the poor second Mrs. Winter.

I've read an awful lot of that stuff, she thought.

She didn't see anyone at all around the building though there were two cars and a service truck parked near the front entrance. She parked her car and went bravely back down the slanting ramp to the front of the building. It wasn't as bad on foot as in the car, but, after all, it was still broad afternoon with the sun streaking across the new concrete. She went through the front door and saw Mr. Bishop sitting at the desk in the lobby, tipped back in his chair, reading a paperback book himself.

"Good afternoon," she said.

The chair banged onto the front legs and Mr. Bishop looked at her, startled.

"I'm sorry," she said.

"Didn't hear you come in," he said. "Reckon I was too interested in my book here."

"I didn't realize you were here in the daytime too," she said.

Mr. Bishop had lumbered to his feet and was watching her. Warily, she thought.

"Well'm, I won't be," he said, "later on. But right now I'm doing two shifts. There's really not enough to do right now for another man. I've got a room here so's I can rest," he added, taking a handkerchief from his pocket and wiping his red face.

"Mr. Bishop," Sara said quietly. "How many families are living in this building?"

"Well, now," he said, embarrassment on his face, "I don't know exactly how many of these apartments are sold. Quite a few, I take it, from what Mr. Snyder tells me. Some of them, like yours, were bought before it was built, and they keep selling, you know."

"I mean how many people have moved in, Mr. Bishop?"

Mr. Bishop was definitely avoiding looking at her now. He gazed down at his paperback as though it might tell him the requisite thing to say. "Well, they's two ladies moved in before going on their European travels," he said slowly. "And Mr. Carter. He's to retire up north and will be . . ."

"I'm the only person who's actually living here. Isn't that right, Mr. Bishop?"

He was defeated, but still he tried. "Well, now, that's mighty temporary, Mrs. Hillstrom," he said. "Mighty temporary. A lot of these folks . . ."

"But right now, today . . . tonight . . . I'm the only one."

"Yessum," he said.

It was, she found, actually a relief to have it said. It was much better to know that it was true than to believe that she was imagining an improbable situation. She smiled at Mr. Bishop. "Well," she said. "I'd thought that, but it seemed rather unlikely to me. So I thought I'd ask."

He seemed vastly relieved at her tone of voice. "It's just one of them unlikely situations," he said. "Another week or so and we'll have so many people in here you'll be falling all over one another and arguing about who's going to use the social room."

"I'm sure we will, Mr. Bishop," she said.

She went across the sun-dappled lobby to the elevator, feeling stoic and prepared against eventualities. But the corridor, when she stepped into its gray and whiteness, seemed longer and quieter, emptier than ever now that she knew for certain there was really nothing behind those doors—nothing alive and breathing anyway. Hopefully not.

Stop it, she told herself, and inserted the key in her lock and opened the door onto afternoon sun and the blue Gulf through the glass doors.

The two packing cases still awaited her and she looked at them gratefully. She wandered slowly into her bedroom and picked up the magazine she'd been reading the night before. I should have stopped and picked up some more, she thought. I should go back to the store now. But the thought of the long trip back down in the elevator, the drive to the shopping center, the drive back, made her feel very tired. She lay down on her twin bed and was immediately asleep.

She woke in surprise to a darkening apartment. It was those drinks, she thought, swimming up into consciousness. I never sleep in the daytime. Never. She got up and looked around her at the shadows falling into the apartment. I forgot to call the drape people, she thought. I should have done that. It'll be much cozier here when I get the drapes up.

She felt loggy and tired still though she'd slept for two hours, and there was a bad taste in her mouth. She went to the bathroom and brushed her teeth vigorously. Then she went to her balcony to enjoy what remained of the sunset. She stood at the railing, looking out at the Gulf with the red sun dropping toward it, the thin line of haze forming at the horizon. Gulls on their homeward route dipped toward her and a line of pelicans came straight at her so that she had to restrain an impulse to duck. She felt very high up and above everything and she looked down at the empty pool below, wondering exactly how high up she really was. She had never been a victim of acrophobia and she was very glad that she never had.

Acrophobia made her think of acrobats and the times she and Howard had gone to Venice to watch the preview performance of the circus. She had always loved the flyers best and she shut her eyes, thinking of them making their daring swoops across the net. Then she remembered a TV show in which the crime had been solved when the detective figured out that it must have been done by acrobats because the criminals had seemingly gone straight up the side of a building and then disappeared into thin air after the crime.

"Oh, God," she said aloud. "No acrobat is coming up here after me. I'm getting silly again."

She made herself enjoy the weak sunset spectacle while it lasted, then go inside and brew coffee and fix another cheese sandwich for a meager supper, telling herself it was all she needed after the restaurant food today.

She had forgotten the solace of tobacco and it was with real pleasure that she remembered the open pack of cigarettes on her kitchen counter. She sat at her kitchen table and watched the smoke rising in front of her, knowing for the first time in her life the comfort derived from the sight of that smoke as well as the taste of it.

She went in gratefully to her packing cases. The first one she opened was the box of miscellaneous things they hadn't been able to discard. She wondered why they hadn't. Nothing in the box was beautiful or useful, or even relevant. There were some guest towels that no one had ever used, but they were real linen and had been given to them by someone who'd been to Ireland. There was a tobacco jar that she'd given Howard the time he took up pipe smoking. That hadn't lasted very long and he'd given the pipes to the yardman; but the tobacco jar remained. There was a silver picture frame that had never looked right with any of their furnishings, but that *was* silver. There was a leather-bound copy of a magazine that had carried an article on Howard's business firm and that had been given to them as a Christmas present. There was a box of junk jewelry that no one had worn in years: class rings and fraternal pins, old charm bracelets, out-of-style earrings. She had kept them because someone had once said that they'd made a beautiful shadow-box arrangement of just that sort of junk and she'd thought that someday, when she had time, she'd do that herself.

All the items depressed her. She closed the box and opened the one that contained Howard's things. She had thought it would be the one to depress her. It hadn't occurred to her those trivial items would be the ones to give her such a sense of complete futility. Or had it been Mary Appleby and alcohol in the bright dining room at the marina? Or was it simply that she couldn't cope, didn't want to cope?

No, it's because I took a nap in the afternoon, she told herself. That never has agreed with me.

Howard had packed his box himself. Some of the items in it, she knew, had been put away in a smaller box for years. It had come south with them this last permanent move. The other things she'd seen him pack.

There were a few books. Though Howard never read much, he liked now and again to dip into an old poetry anthology he'd kept from college, and he had a one-volume Shakespeare, a dictionary, and a battered copy of *Huckleberry Finn*. Automatically she took the books into the bedroom and put them on his bedside table. Then she stood still in the middle of the room and stared at them. The thought of them lying there, untouched, unread, was dreadful. She put them on her bed table. That bothered her too, and she realized she was holding her wrist again, a dull cold feeling in her chest. She took them back to the living room and put them on the bottom shelf with her crystal. But they didn't look right there. They made the crystal look frivolous. And the crystal made them look even older and shabbier than they were.

"I don't know what to do with them," she said out loud, and was sorry. The sound of her own voice filled her with self-pity. She had an impulse to throw the books against the wall, or over the balcony rail outside. She left them on the shelf and went back to the box. She unpacked two golf trophies. They were a relief to her. There was a place for them, already decided. On each side of the kitchen door there was a small alcove. She and Howard had both thought they would be just right for the trophies. She placed them there, pleased with the look of solidarity they gave that corner of the room.

The golf trophies belonged here as much as the new furniture, because Howard had only seriously taken up golf since he had decided to move permanently to Florida. He'd always played, but halfheartedly. It was only here that it had become important enough to him to win trophies. His clubs were at the club. She wondered if Jack would like them. There were so many things she should have asked Jack about. But everything had happened so quickly. It was only now, in this strange building, that time had stopped.

She let herself look at her watch then. It was nine o'clock.

A vagrant corner of her mind said, It's still too early to get scared. She answered it indignantly. But tonight I'm not going to *be* scared.

Howard's fishing clothes were in the box, the disreputable old hat and jacket that he had always been afraid she'd throw away and that she'd never had any intention of throwing away. That was just one of the things she'd never been able to make him understand about her. His new Shakespeare reel was there too, and his favorite tackle in a little tin box. The big tackle box was still in the trunk of the car. Downstairs in that tomblike mass of concrete.

She shivered and searched further in the box. His college degree, still in the envelope it had been mailed to him in after he'd failed to show up for graduation—one of his favorite stories. Three service plaques from the firm with gold on oak citing him for superior salesmanship. And in the bottom of the crate the flat box that contained the things he'd brought from Minneapolis. It occurred to her that whatever was in that box was probably something important only to Howard himself, as her crystal was important to her, and that maybe she shouldn't even open it.

But she did open it. And for a long time she sat in surprise, turning over the few items. Unlike the things she had unpacked, none of them were anything she would have imagined Howard keeping at all. They were all so unlike the Howard she knew and had lived with that they seemed lugubrious, something someone else had collected for him and decided he should keep purely to rattle and frighten Sara when it was too late for her to know what to do about it.

There was a stack of letters from Howie, dating all the way back to camp and prep school. She had never thought Howard had kept any letter of Howie's. The two of them had always seemed to have such difficulty communicating in any way. But there they were. There was a snapshot of herself in a bathing suit, taken the first year they'd ever come to Florida. It wasn't even a good picture, she thought, frowning at it. He hadn't kept a good picture of her at all. Her wedding picture, the few portraits, were in the family album underneath her dressing table. Why on earth would he have that tacky old snapshot in his box?

There was also his old Swiss Army knife that they'd bought in Jamaica the year he'd won the company trip, and there was the set of brushes she'd given him for their tenth wedding anniversary and that he'd always said were too good to use because they had silver backs. She'd always suspected him of losing them on a business trip, though she'd never mentioned them to him after their seeming disappearance.

She sat there, staring at the things in the box with an intense unhappiness. She picked up the snapshot again. Suddenly she seemed to smell salt and sand in a way you were never able to smell it after you lived beside it. The way it had smelled the day of that long-ago photograph. She could feel the Gulf breeze on slightly burned skin and the scratch of sand on her legs, and the unbelievably hot sun between her shoulder blades.

They had eaten raw oysters with raw onion and horseradish for lunch, something new for both of them. She wondered suddenly how long it had been since she had eaten something new. How long since she'd had her picture taken? How long since Howard had smiled at her the way he had that day? And said something just a little risqué about her legs . . . because it was Florida and beautiful and a free, in-between vacation time that didn't come often. That finally never came any more.

Why? she thought. And put the thought aside with the photograph. Put it away with what she knew to be too accustomed ease. Something better not thought about, not just tonight, but for a long long time.

There was one other item in the box and she picked it up tentatively, as though it might explode in her face. It was a book of poetry, a small leather-bound volume. Flipping to the title page, she saw that it was Edna Millay's sonnets. Scrawled on the endpaper in French were the words *Bonjour et A'voir*. She stared at the scrawl, thinking, I am getting strange here alone. That looks like Moira's handwriting. How ridiculous.

She remembered times in the past when she'd thought crazy things like that, found theater stubs and thought Howard had taken someone else somewhere before she remembered the week they'd seen a play themselves, having ugly and useless suspicions that made life a silly hell and that accomplished nothing. She slammed the things all back into the box, rose to her feet, and froze in horror.

There was a sound in the apartment next door.

For a moment she couldn't move at all. She didn't even breathe. Then, without knowing she'd done it, she had stumbled across the opened boxes and reached the intercom on the wall. She unfroze to find her hand hovering over the button in mindless panic. She pushed it. For a long horrible moment nothing happened. Then Mr. Bishop's voice, earthy, southern, matter-of-fact through the tinny distortion of the intercom, "Yes, Mrs. Hillstrom?"

Immediately she felt silly. What could she possibly say to the man? There's someone in the empty apartment next door? Would you please come up, I heard a noise? No. She remembered her panic at the sound of the air conditioner changing pitch last night. This, too, was probably some everyday sound of an apartment building she wasn't accustomed to yet.

"Mrs. Hillstrom?" Mr. Bishop said again.

"Mr. Bishop," she said, fighting to keep her voice level. She looked at her watch. Nine-thirty. Still too early for fear. "I was wondering," she said, "when you're going to fill the pool."

She could hear the relief in his voice. "Well, now," he said happily. "Isn't that funny? I just today talked to Mr. Snyder about that and he said he thought we should go on and fill it now. In fact, I've called the pool men to come in tomorrow. Funny, isn't it? You thinking of that too. But seemed to me, with all this dry weather, it might be nice for you. Specially as the water's been right rough in the Gulf lately."

She could hear her own breath, still too rapid and shallow, and she tried not to breathe into the intercom. "How very nice," she said.

"Well, good then," he said. "Everything else all right?"

"Oh yes," she said. "Everything's fine."

"Well, just buzz if you need anything," he said.

The voice clicked off and she visualized him going back to his paperback book. She wondered what it was.

Still she stood there, close beside the mechanical comfort of the intercom, trying to recapture and place that sound. It could have been the thermostat next door, of course. That apartment might belong to the lady who'd gone to Europe. It could have been her refrigerator cutting off or on. Because she knew that the sound had come from the other side of her living room wall. It had not been in this apartment. It had not been in the corridor.

She moved, very slowly, around the packing cases and stood where she had been when she heard it. Yes. It had come from her left, from the other side of the living room wall which was the wall of the adjoining apartment. She was quite certain of it. She hadn't been in the other apartment so she wasn't sure which of its rooms backed onto her living room. If, for instance, she'd known it was the kitchen, the refrigerator explanation would have been more plausible. She gave a small whimper. She knew quite well, in spite of all her sensible rationalizations, the sound hadn't been a mechanical sound at all. It had been a woman's laugh. A small laugh, half secretive, half smothered, but a laugh.

Her heart had begun to pound again, but she made herself quietly cross the room and lean her ear against the blank betraying wall. She could hear nothing at all. Though she stood there for what seemed a long time the only sound was the sound of her own breathing, much louder than necessary to insure air in her lungs.

"I won't, I won't," she said, and flung herself away from the wall. She walked across the room and loudly dragged the boxes to the hall closet.

The hall wasn't much of a hall, only a small square separating the bedrooms and bath from the rest of the apartment. The hall closet, however, was the biggest one in the apartment, meant, no doubt, as a cloak room as well as a storage place. There were a good many things in it already, clothes and fishing equipment, a few household items she hadn't found a place for yet. She wrestled the boxes in beneath the clothes and slammed the door.

She enjoyed the resounding noise, comforted by her own temerity, before she began to tremble, and realized she'd bitten down on the inside of her lower lip until it was bleeding.

She forced her mind away from the empty apartment next door and back to the boxes. She even tried to recover her feeling of shock and suspicion at finding the book of poems. But she knew that it was no use. You couldn't care about the petty toils of the ugly human emotions like jealousy when you were terrified.

And she was terrified. The knowledge of the foolishness of it didn't change the fact. She was shaking, her heart was pounding, her mouth was dry. No matter what she told herself about reality she knew reality to be that laugh from the apartment next door.

All right, she told herself. You're scared. But the door is locked and the windows are locked. Or are they?

It amazed her that she hadn't thought of that before and she began methodically, though in haste, to check all the windows. A part of herself looked on and knew it was nonsense, another part instructed her in haste and prudence and method. They were all locked.

She paused in the kitchen and her eye fell on the cigarettes. She lit one and stood in the glaring light inhaling deeply, for the first time. Now, she told herself. Think.

She sat down at the table and tried to do just that. In the first place, why should she be afraid of a woman laughing? Only, of course, because she was laughing in a place where no one should be. Where, so Mr. Bishop said, no one was.

But she had heard. So there was some explanation. She did not believe in psychic phenomenon; and even if there were some such thing it wouldn't occur in a brand-new modern condominium. Ghosts favored old and dark and battered houses; ghosts lived where people had lived before. They didn't haunt a place that still smelled of new plaster and paint and was empty of former life.

If the laugh were not a ghost, it could be in her own head. That, however, was extremely unlikely. She wasn't that imaginative, had never been. If her mind wasn't one of depth, it wasn't one of fantasies either.

No, someone had laughed. That left many possibilities. The lady traveling in Europe could have come back unannounced. That was the likeliest explanation. She might call downstairs and ask Mr. Bishop and he would tell her, Yes, in fact, the lady had moved in. But no, he would have mentioned it when he talked about the pool. He'd said, *You* might enjoy it. And it had been a singular *you*. All right, so it wasn't her. A new tenant could have moved in. But he would also have mentioned that. No, it was—it had to be—someone illicit. And that, of course, was the reason she was so very afraid.

She felt better just having the thought. She went back to the living room and stood for a long time listening. But there was only the sigh of her own appliances, keeping her world at the acceptable levels for luxurious life.

Her heart had slowed, she was breathing almost normally again. She even felt like making herself a cup of coffee and went to the kitchen to do it before she remembered that caffeine did tend to june one up, and that certainly with the adrenalin already in her system she didn't need that.

She stood indecisively in her kitchen before she remembered the bottle of sherry. Of course. A glass of that, sipped slowly. She opened the unfamiliar bottle and selected a pretty glass. The little movements made her feel better and she went back to the living room and sat in a chair with her ankles crossed primly and sipped at the sherry as though she were attending a party.

No one laughed again.

She allowed herself a deep sigh, freeing her lungs completely for the first time since she'd heard the sound. The sherry and the comfort of the big chair lulled her until suddenly an explanation, bright and ripping as sunlight, occurred to her.

Mr. Theodore Snyder, that strange and upsetting young man, wearing his sneakers and sideburns and pretending to be in authority. Of course. He was probably using the empty apartment as a place of assignation. That was just the sort of thing a young man like that might do. He would think it funny.

The thought left her with a feeling of cheerful indignation. If that were all. Heavens. It was even comforting to think of the two of them, Theodore Snyder and some strange girl in the poor lady-in-Europe's bed.

Ten o'clock. She went to her bedroom and turned on the radio.

Its murmur made a steady background of comfort as she undressed and got ready for bed—though she didn't take her bath. The idea of getting into the tub didn't appeal to her, even now with her feeling of relief at the thought of company, however degenerate, next door.

She got her magazine and cigarettes and got into bed, determined to read all the articles tonight and tomorrow to buy something new to read tomorrow night. She didn't want to think about tomorrow night. She thought instead about going to the drugstore newsstand in the morning. In the morning. Yes. With the bright sunlight and the newly-filled pool to sit beside. She looked up from her magazine. The dressing table was opposite the foot of the bed so that she could see herself in the tilted mirror, a long dim object under the sheets, leaning back on pillows, the face indistinct and blurred even with the lamplight shining on it. She jumped involuntarily. There was something corpselike about that swaddled body. Her mind threw up a jumbled sequence of thought: bed, and birth, and death, and procreation mixed in a sick mélange. She threw the sheets back and hastily went to move the dressing table and mirror down the wall opposite the empty twin bed.

She sank back into bed, panting. She picked up her magazine and read doggedly an article on schools, another on diets, and another on sex. Her mind registered the words of all the articles, but not the sense. The sense seemed to her to be all nonsense, a lot of talk about nothing except compromise in the face of confusion.

The radio still murmured on the table. She turned it off, realizing that she was listening again. She had, she knew, been listening all the time she was scanning the printed words. Listening for some sign from next door, some confirmation of the liaison taking place there: a commode flushing, a movement across the floor, a creak of bedspring. Even another laugh. But there had been nothing.

I'll hear better with the radio off, she thought. I may even be able to hear them when they leave. She wondered if she could hear the elevator from in here, but she knew she couldn't. That sound was too slight, too mechanically perfect. The elevators here sighed their way up and down the shaft. They didn't rumble or grumble like the elevator in that old building they'd lived in the first year they were married, the one that used to wake everybody in the house when someone came in late at night. No, these elevators were painlessly silent. Like everything morbid. The rubber-tired wheels of death. In the midst of a loud civilization. The idea machine in her mind came up with a new thought. *Perhaps everyone makes so much noise to close out those silent sounds of death.*

There you go, she told herself. Maybe you had better turn the radio back on.

But she didn't. She lay on her pillows, quite still, listening. And after a while she began to hear the sound of her own heart beating again.

She got up and put on her robe and slippers, pulling the sash of the robe tightly around her as though cinching the girth of armor. She felt better in the robe, less vulnerable. She felt good enough to go into the living room and turn on the light and stand looking at her shelves of crystal. The pieces on the shelf where she'd placed Howard's books seemed out of line and she stooped down to rearrange the gazelles. Her hand wasn't steady and she clinked one of them against the other. She set it down quickly, looking in horror to see if she had chipped one of the delicate ears. It looked all right and she ran her hand carefully over it, feeling for a crack.

Then she heard the second sound from the apartment next door. Not movement, not a commode flushing, nor a closing door. Something far stranger, and terrifying. It was a subtle clinking, almost an echo of the sound the gazelles had made.

Her heart stopped. She knew it stopped because when it began again there was a sharp pain under her breast. And for the first time since Howard had died she realized that it had been her heart that bore the scar. Dr. Richmond had discovered it in a routine examination, and he had told her that at some time, unknown, unremarked by her, she had had a coronary. Which meant, of course, she could and probably would, have another.

Only she hadn't. And Howard had.

But I'm not having one now, she thought. My heart is pounding away, but perfectly normally. I'm just scared out of my wits. And for no reason. No reason. They were pouring a drink in there. That's what they were doing. There is nothing in the world frightening about somebody pouring a drink.

She straightened up slowly and went again to that inner wall and listened, but there was nothing. No voices, no movement, no sound at all in the night. She tiptoed nonetheless toward the intercom and stood with one finger poised over it for a long moment before turning away.

She couldn't call Mr. Bishop again. It was too late, and she'd already called once. She looked at her watch. It was eleven forty-five. The time they used to have to be back in the dorm at college. And now, she thought wryly, they keep boys in there all night. It had said in the magazine article that all the girls said it was innocent and social. Why then, she thought, was it evil and awful if we stayed out past eleven forty-five? And, my goodness, that was only on weekends. It was ten forty-five during the week.

Howard used to say, "We'd better hurry. Remember the devil pops out and directs all your actions at exactly ten forty-six. We've no time to spare."

Well, it was eleven forty-six now. And everybody said the devil didn't exist any more. Not the one with pointed ears like the gazelles. Though, if he did, he probably had sideburns and sneakers and a shirt left open to the navel.

Oh hush, hush, she told her own mind. Stop it all. She turned with determination and went to the kitchen for the sherry bottle. She poured into the sticky glass she'd left sitting on the sink and sat down. "They're drinking," she said. "I'll drink too."

It was with a shock that she realized how warming the sherry was, gulped the way she'd just gulped it, rather than sipped. It gave her a momentary false flush of courage, an almost To-the-devil-who-doesn't-exist with you, for the people next door. They were keeping her awake. Carrying on in someone else's apartment, carrying on in her life.

The scared, trembling woman vanished from her kitchen and was replaced by normal indignant Sara Hillstrom. If anyone was next door disturbing her rest it was because they were breaking a law. No one belonged there. She'd simply go next door and knock and tell them to go away.

She felt emboldened by the idea, and more normal than she'd felt since she had first entered this apartment. All her fears and imaginings were unreal, the product of too little sleep, the aftermath of Howard's death and trying to readjust to a life without him. Bits and pieces of the magazine articles she'd read came to reassure her. Everyone had bad moments and thoughts. But all could be overcome by simple planning.

She went to the bedroom and lit a cigarette almost cavalierly. She went to the dressing table mirror and tucked in the straying wisps of hair. She set her mouth in a purposeful line and nodded briskly at her own image.

She drew disdainfully on the cigarette. She reassured herself by thinking of the time she'd had to tell the people next door in the old apartment to stop drinking and carousing all night. Howard hadn't wanted her to say anything, but it was his sleep that they had been disturbing. She'd been very plain about it. There had been no trouble either. The man who'd come to the door had been very sheepish and apologetic. And the noise had stopped. That night and thereafter.

She would simply do the same thing now. If they persisted she'd call Mr. Bishop and let him deal with them. She really didn't want to get them into any trouble. If they'd just quit bothering her she wouldn't tell on them. She wasn't that sort of moral prude. She just didn't want to be disturbed. That was all.

She knew, deep underneath her Dutch courage and her

artificial calm, that this was not a situation where you told the carousing people next door to calm down the party; knew that she'd only heard a smothered laugh and a clink of crystal. But she didn't want to let herself know that. Her body, needing action, any kind of action, propelled her forward to the front door where she took the chain off the hook, turned the knob, and stepped into the hall.

The hallway gave her momentary pause. It looked as it always did, long and gray and quiet, unnaturally quiet, unnaturally lit. But she kept on, purposefully setting her corduroy slippers onto the gray carpet and approaching the door next door.

She lifted her hand and knocked. At the last moment, some of her resolution was going and the knock, instead of sounding loud and peremptory, seemed scared and apologetic, so she tried it again almost simultaneously. Then she waited.

Nothing happened at all except that she began to have a cold feeling in the middle of her back. She could no more have looked over her shoulder than she could have flown like a flyer off her balcony. She knocked again, louder. Surprisingly, and to her horror, the door swung softly open and inward under her hand.

Chapter 5

She was trapped in a moment of complete stasis. She could neither go forward into the apartment nor turn back into the empty hall. The feeling in the middle of her back denoted some-one or something staring at her from the door of a silently open-ing elevator, the apartment in front of her might denote . . . anything. The horror of what might be behind overcame the horror of going forward. She went through the open door.

She took two tentative steps into the entry and paused. It was completely dark. She stood still, letting her eyes adjust. It was still dark. There was only a faint gleam from the front windows.

Something propelled her forward and she went on, finding her-self standing in the middle of the living room, darkness and silence around her. In front of her was the patch of light from the outside and she could discern through the glass doors an empty balcony.

She felt herself to be a horrid, beating, pulsing animal entity in the midst of emptiness and silence. She wanted to admonish her heart and blood and breath and glands to hush up, to stop making all those unbelievably loud and unnecessary noises that would perforce call up something, someone, to deal with them;

if only to stop their horrid clatter and chatter in what should have been complete silence. She tried to direct her ears outward to hear if there were any other animal bodies making the strained and straining noises of keeping themselves alive in space. But all she could hear was her own traitorous breath and blood. She held the breath, but the blood still pounded in her ears.

She cut her eyes to right and left, hoping they wouldn't make a tremendous noise with their liquid sliding.

The room seemed to be completely empty. It smelled faintly of paint and plaster just as her apartment had done before she had moved in. She could feel the carpet under her feet. But there was no furniture in the room. It was as empty as the hallway outside.

Her mind freed itself of its animal existence and told her that didn't mean anything. If someone were using the apartment illegally they wouldn't need furniture. Just having a thought released her and she moved gently and quietly sideways until she fetched up at the door into the kitchen. It was to her left; which meant, of course, the kitchen did back onto her apartment. She cut her eyes again and saw the bulk of the refrigerator beside the sink. It was silent, silent as only a refrigerator that has never been plugged into the current can be. The sink was silent too, no drip of water, no gurglings from the drainpipe. She put her head all the way around the door and saw the bulk of dead appliances just barely gleaming in the faint light from the uncurtained living room.

For a long moment she stood still again, listening. And after a while there was a sound. A faint sound, ghostly, unconnected with anything until it stopped with a small bump and she realized it had been the front door which she had left open swinging to behind her.

She was committed now. She was in here. With whatever or whoever else was. Then she swayed against the wall and felt the first gasp of real terror. Because maybe somebody had come in that door behind her and it hadn't swung to of its own accord at all.

She knew this wasn't true. She knew it could not be true, because from where she was leaning she could see the sweep of the living room and there was no one at all in it. They couldn't have gotten in and hidden away in the one moment she peered into the kitchen.

Unless, of course, they were standing in the entry by the intercom, just out of sight around the entry archway.

The thought was so terrible there was nothing to do with it but look. Like looking into the closets before bed. She took the three steps needed across the floor and looked. There was nothing there.

She could see the intercom box in the wall and she wondered if she could contact Mr. Bishop from here; if the boxes were all hooked up or if only the one in her own apartment—so very far away down that treacherous corridor—could and did work. She knew she hadn't the strength to find out. The three steps across the living room had been all that was in her for the moment.

What she wanted to do was sink down on the carpet under her feet, fold herself into a ball, and crouch there, safe, at least, from what she might see. A child, hiding under the covers and thinking that if he couldn't see he couldn't be seen. Peekaboo, she'd say to Howie, and pull the covers off, and he'd shriek.

My God, she thought. You scare them when you do that. You're scaring them. We scare all our children to death before they know what fear is, and we think we're playing games with them. We grab at them and yell, *I gotcha.* And they repay us with shrieks of laughter, and we never consider that it is hysteria.

She realized she was praying in an insane litany. *Please don't let anyone say, I gotcha. Please, God, don't let anyone say, Peekaboo.*

After a while she became aware of another sound beside that of her shallow breathing and her racing blood. It was another rhythmic sound and for that reason it didn't frighten her. She knew it to be normal and understood, part of the world of order. It was her watch, ticking away steadily and calmly, much more regularly and competently than her heart. She felt grateful to it. It was a friend, telling her that time was, is, would be. That it was passing and would pass and that it didn't matter what one did, it went right on at its inexorable steady rate; that day would come, and night again, and day, and, finally, an end.

It gave her courage in the dark and emptiness and she was able to think coherently. There were still the bedrooms and bath. And the closets. She had forgotten the closets.

She knew that she couldn't possibly look into them without turning on a light. She thought, for the first time, of the reason she had actually come into this place. She had been going to surprise malefactors, send away a couple indulging in illicit acts in an illicit place. She had a sudden picture of opening a closet door to find the couple among the clothing, naked and terrified, as terrified as she was.

It struck her as funny and she almost giggled. It turned the world back into a place in which she could survive. She walked across the room and flicked the light switch, discovering, to her surprise, she didn't really expect it to come on. But it did, flooding the empty room with light, showing up its emptiness.

She knew in the moment of flicking the switch that she was the only thing in the apartment. She felt it, down in those places where the blood murmured through the cells. But she looked anyway. Into the empty kitchen again, in the storage closet, in the two bedrooms, the bath, and all the closets.

It was the emptiest place in the universe. There was nothing, not even the dust of time.

Not just no people, but no trappings of people. No furniture, no clothing, not anything. The closets were small square boxes of freshly painted space. The bathroom fixtures had never felt the flow of water. The rooms, since the painters had left with their buckets and the carpenters with their leftover tacks, had not known the presence of human flesh.

She found that, rather than relief, she was feeling a faint annoyance. She had wanted to find somebody in this apartment, no matter who, no matter how degenerate. They would have been people, human beings in this ridiculous honeycomb of steel and concrete, someone besides herself to breathe and gurgle and beat with the insistence of living flesh.

Instead there was emptiness and blankness. Here, in all the rest of the building, maybe in all the world. She was so completely alone as to make civilization absurd.

She thought of how she'd hated such sounds as motorcycles passing loudly in the night; and she knew that right now that sound would have been infinitely comforting and dear.

She went through the empty rooms turning out the lights. She went to the door and opened it and went into the empty hall. She walked toward her own door and opened that, and knew at least the comfort of light and the smells of human occupancy: tobacco smoke and the mustiness of the opened boxes and the lingering smell of coffee from supper, all seeming more intense than she would have imagined. She closed her door and bolted it and affixed the chain.

Only then, standing with her back to her occupied rooms and her empty glass doors, did she realize she'd been out of the apartment and left the door unlocked, that anything or anyone could have come in while she was prowling the emptiness next door.

Anything or anyone could be waiting.

She leaned her head against the white panels of the closed and locked door and allowed herself to cry for one small space.

She cried because she knew that only a second before she had been longing for the humanness of anyone, even a murderer or thief, any crazed and impossible fate, as long as it involved another human being. And that now, a human being behind her in her tiny living space was the one thing she feared most in all the world.

She turned her wet face and looked at the comfort of the call box on the wall. She thought of solid, ridiculous Mr. Bishop reading his paperback book. She thought that he was so far away in the subterranean depths below that the hand could grasp and smother before he could even answer the intercom, much less lumber to the elevator and come in rescue. *Gotcha Sara. Gotcha. Peekaboo.*

She turned in resignation and began the now familiar search of the too familiar rooms, the balcony silent and dead with white iron furniture like the entry of a funeral parlor, the kitchen with its monsters of steel and chrome and hidden plumbing, the bedrooms—under the beds, of course—the bathroom—behind the shower curtain, the closets—feel along the cluttered floors.

Nobody here but you, Sara. Nobody here but you.

She sat down on the edge of her rumpled bed and the enormity of what she had just done swept over her. The fact of that fearless, then fearful, sojourn down the hall and into and through that cavern of emptiness next door, leaving her nest open and vulnerable to whatever might have entered, herself vulnerable not only to what might have been next door but to what might have awaited her here on her return. It had been madness. Actual madness. A momentary falling into the trap of forgetfulness that awaits us all.

As long as she stayed here, inside this lighted series of rooms, locked in and lulled by the miracles of modern life, she was safe. It was herself she had to fear, fleeing heedlessly into empty hallways and apartments, opening locked doors, pushing into hidden rooms.

Here was the comfort and bulk of furniture and appliance, the soothing comfort of air conditioner and refrigerator, of water from the tap. The coziness of bedside lamp and radio, the telephone standing mute but sentient inside its hall alcove. She had only to pick it up and call. Call anyone anywhere in all the world. Call Howie far away in a silly country, call Betty Jane and Jack in Minneapolis, call Mary Appleby Carrol at the Twin Towers, call the police, the fire department, the F.B.I. Call anyone at all and say the one word, Help. Communicate and receive. The insubstantial wafer of life.

Except that the phone hadn't been turned on yet. The phone company had said, "sometime this week." Nevertheless she walked toward it, staring at it as though it were a black monster crouching in her alcove. My God, she thought. What if it should ring?

With a feeling of complete despair she picked it up and heard, with a thrill of surprise and joy, the steady humming of the dial tone. They'd turned it on after all. She *could* call.

She looked, with the rueful and automatic gesture, at her watch. It was one o'clock now. It was far too late. Too late to call anyone without a reason. And to whisper, Help, is never any reason. The telephone was not invented for that word, no matter what the sugar-voiced girls on the TV advertisements said. The telephone was invented to transmit invitations, and loving messages, and cheerful chat; to make a dental date or solicit subscriptions. The telephone had no direct connection with God.

With the thought, shamefacedly, exasperatedly, and with a touch of self-irony, she looked up the number and dialed the Dial-A-Prayer.

The line clicked, hummed, faltered, and a cheerful mechanical voice said, "The number you have reached is not in service at this time. This is a recorded announcement."

She stood for a moment, the receiver still at her ear, and began to laugh. She leaned weakly against the wall, gasping at the absurdity of everything. Then she put the receiver back on the hook and told herself that what she'd better do was make a cup of tea.

It was the one thing she could think of that had a cheerful normal sound to it. A cup of tea to chase the horrors. The backbone of the British Empire. A little backbone for Sara Hillstrom in sunny Florida.

When she got to the kitchen she realized that there wasn't any tea in the apartment, but she didn't let it stop her. She would have coffee as though it were tea, in the pretty tea service with the silver strainer that had belonged to Howard's grandmother. All the things were here, of course, because they were the kind of things one saved, even when whittling down their lives to the bare essentials. No one got rid of the china or the silver tea service, even if they left them to gather dust and quietly tarnish on the pantry shelf.

She arranged the tea set on a tray and brewed the coffee. She remembered her cigarettes and went to the bedroom for them and their added comfort. She got linen place mat and napkin from the drawer. She made herself a little British outpost in Darkest Africa and arranged it neatly on her dining table.

Perhaps I should dress for tea, she thought, still feeling faintly humorous. It wouldn't do to go native now. If I dressed I could buzz Mr. Bishop and ask him up. Tell him to bring Mr. Snyder along if he is here. Have a coffee break for the residents of the Triton. She poured into her china cup and the teapot clinked against the thin gold rim.

With the sound all the real terror she'd been placating and keeping in abeyance with the rituals of phone and coffee, even with the ritual of searching underneath the beds, came creeping back across the brightly lit room and the shining tea set.

She had gone into that apartment next door for a reason. She hadn't simply fled in panic to that empty place. She'd gone there to investigate a noise. A clink of crystal and a woman's laugh. Distinct and ordinary sounds of life. And the apartment had been as dead and empty as a tomb.

I did not imagine it, she told herself, sipping coffee. I heard it, with my ears and not my mind. Someone, somewhere, laughed, and someone clinked a glass. If not there, somewhere else. I heard it.

She got up and went to stand in the middle of her living room. It still seemed to her that the sounds had come from behind the wall between the apartments. But she thought about it, tried to reorient the sensation. Told herself it could have been in the hall. Or maybe from another apartment; there were others to the back of this floor. It could have been some acoustical trick, the sound coming through the air-conditioning vents or the plumbing even. Surely she'd heard of that. It could have come from the beach below. Someone could have been there, having a late picnic on the property. That Theodore and his girl friend, Mr. Bishop, errant teen-agers. Oh, certainly it could have been almost anything.

The coffee, when she went back to it, was cold. She poured more from the pot and forced herself to drink it. She took the cup into the living room and sat in the big chair, staring blindly at the crystal animals animated into antic life by all the lights she'd left on.

I was looking into Howard's things, she told herself. I wasn't afraid at all when I heard the laugh. I wasn't thinking of anything that could have frightened me. In fact, I was thinking about that book.

In the thought she knew she was reluctant to pursue it. What if she followed it through and the laughter came again? What if she then moved to touch her crystal treasures and the clinking came again? What then? Already she had exhausted the possibilities of the place next door. There was nowhere she could tell Mr. Bishop to look if she should call him. Like Dial-A-Prayer, the number was not in service. Nothing was. Mary Appleby had said that about the Triton. Not in service. But she was here. And tomorrow they were going to fill the swimming pool.

Tomorrow. She looked at her watch. It was two o'clock. The really bad time. The dreadful time. But close to reprieve. Two more hours. One could breathe at four because the world would be getting ready to begin again. So, only two more hours. There was no one in this apartment. The door was locked, the lights were on. She'd turn on the radio and listen to the all-night disc jockey. Anyone could stand anything for two hours. Even the possibility of not knowing where sounds came from. Or why.

And tomorrow. Tomorrow, she'd simply move back to her old

apartment. Tomorrow she'd give up this castle of empty boxes and go back home.

The thought was so happy and unexpected she almost hugged herself. Of course. She didn't have to stay here. She'd sell the thing and live somewhere else on the proceeds. She had enough to keep her going in the old place until a buyer appeared. She didn't let herself think about the fact that she was the only occupant in the building. She refused to let herself think of that. Reprieve seemed simple and certain. She'd sell out and go back to a place where people came and went, but were most certainly always, at least some of them, there.

There was only tonight to get through. And that was easy now. Anybody could get through just one night.

She knew that she had had that thought before. She remembered when.

The night that Howie had run away. August. With the stars enormous in the northern sky and September just a few short weeks away, the thought of chill and cold Minneapolis winter already hovering in the hot and humid, tornado-making wind.

They had gotten Howie into a very good eastern boarding school, and she had thought he wanted to go. She'd thought he loved the idea. She'd thought a lot of fond and foolish things.

It had been a Thursday night, the night he always went over to practice ball with Herman Birch. So that she'd figured he'd come in late and tired and hungry, and she'd made a chocolate pie and been sure there was some cold roast beef left. And Howard had grumbled, as usual, because she'd kept some back.

Then it had been nine o'clock, and ten, and eleven. And Howard had come in from the den where he'd been reading and said, "Well, where the hell is he? It's nearly midnight."

And she'd said, "Should I call Mrs. Birch?"

And Howard had looked at her strangely and said, "Let's wait till twelve."

It had amazed her that he hadn't been angry, that his voice

had been very quiet and still. She'd thought, My God, he's keeping something from me.

Then it had been twelve-thirty. And Howard came back in and said, "I'll call."

Later, of course, he'd yelled at her. And accused her of always having been too soft on Howie. He'd threatened to disown him and let him find out what the world was all about and how damned hard it was to turn an honest dime. But what she remembered now, waiting for dawn in this silent place, was the quietness in his voice when he'd said, "Let's wait till twelve."

At one they'd called the police. And while they talked to the tall young man in blue those words had kept running helter-skelter through her mind. *Anybody can get through just one night.* Because by morning there would be something. News impossible to live with, or a reprieve.

But at dawn there had been nothing but emptiness. It had been three whole days, three nights of just-one-night before Howie had turned up on the doorstep, sheepish and belligerent and afraid. By that time Howard had taken off himself and left her to it. That last night had been as lonely and fearful as this night tonight.

Well, Sara told herself, sitting straight and frightened in the big blue chair. You said then, when you lived through that, that never again would you find it hard to live through anything.

Only, she thought, the body doesn't know that. It pays no attention at all to the pledges of the mind. It keeps on manufacturing its adrenalin for emergencies and driving you to fight or flee.

Howard had flown during that long-ago crisis. But, like Howie, he had come back. As sheepishly as Howie himself. And in the nights that followed, even in the midst of thanksgiving that neither was maimed or tortured or mercifully dead, she'd had to think that both had run from her. And had to put that thought away because nobody wants to be the thing run from. Everybody wants to be the sheltering arms.

And yet, she thought, staring at the blank wall in front of her,

Howard kept all those letters from Howie. There they are now in that pasteboard box, that box that contains all the real Howard left anywhere in this world. Letters from Howie. Who finally went on to school and came home to harangue us with his ideas and dreams and went on to marry Ely with her bare and dirty feet. Howie, who is now half a world away with a son of his own to threaten his peace in an unpeaceful world.

And he kept a photograph of you in a bathing suit. You a little too plump, you embarrassed by all the freedom of salt and sand. But you. And he kept a small black book of poetry with an inscription in a bold and familiar hand.

Don't think about that, her mind shrieked. Don't think about that. That is when you heard . . . She listened. She looked at her watch. It was two-thirty. Thirty blessed minutes had flown somewhere. There was no sound but the watch, ticking the dark away. No one laughed. No one performed strange acts in empty apartments. It was going to be all right for another hour. And then it would be almost four o'clock.

I'll wash the dishes, she thought. I'll tidy up.

It was such a normal thought, such a usual thing for Sara Hillstrom, that she was surprised to find her body fighting the idea. I'm tired, it told her. I'm completely worn out. I've done enough for this twenty-four hours. I've done enough for this one day.

But she got up anyway and wearily, tiredly, knowing she'd have sighed if there had been anyone to sigh to, cleared her brave tea set from the table, washed up in the new sink, sprinkled the washing powder and scrubbed the stainless steel, wiped the dishes and put them away.

I wonder, she thought, how many dishes I've washed in my life? By hand, by machine, by the expedient of extorting some hired girl into doing it? How many in the years? It's an awful thought.

She'd read somewhere once that washing dishes by hand was soothing, that it gave one a feeling of security and peace, that it allowed you to think as the water ran warm and cleansing over your hands. For herself, she thought not. It allowed her not to think. Thinking, she had found, wasn't always a happy thing.

She had had to think a lot during those three days when first Howie, then Howard, had gone out of her life. She'd thought more in those three days than ever before or since. And truth to tell she hadn't liked it. She wasn't at all sure, then or now, that it had accomplished anything at all.

Certainly it hadn't brought them back to her. Whatever had done that had been something completely out of her hands.

Maybe it all is, she thought, hanging up the damp dish towel. Out of our hands, that is.

And if that were so, why, for God sakes, should any of us ever be afraid? If fate is fixed and sure and firm, how can anything frighten us? What will be, will be, and fleeing, fearing, even fighting, means nothing whatsoever in the scheme of things.

She looked at her watch and saw that it was three. She was really in very good shape. The night was going rapidly toward an end. She had ascertained that there was nothing next door. And now, after washing dishes, she was not about to admit that that fact could frighten more than anything. Soon the sun would come up. The day would begin in all its myriad ways. Cars would run on the roads, people would walk away and toward, hungry stomachs would be demanding breakfast, bosses would be demanding work. All the people of the world would be up and out and doing.

And she could go and live again in the little apartment on the shaded side street. She could leave the tower of empty boxes and never never come back to it again.

She would even be able to visit Mary Appleby. Knowing no Bluebeard kept a place on the wall for Sara's head, she could dare the empty spaces of someone else's tower dwelling. The drawbridge would be firmly down and she could walk back across it into life.

Listen, she said to the silent apartment around her. You have nothing to do with me at all. You have only been a place where

I've spent a few bad hours. And that is over now. I'm going home.

She saw in her mind's eye the harrowed, nerve-wracked woman who had actually, in what could only be described as need, given in to all the shibboleths and dialed the Dial-A-Prayer. Knowing, even before it had happened, that the recorded voice was all she was ever likely to receive.

She went quite calmly to her bedroom, turning off lights as she went. She gave only token obeisance to the crystal creatures, she gave only token obeisance to the locks and bars.

In bed she watched, for a moment only, the light from the bathroom door and its accompanying shadows. She turned off the bedside lamp, she slid beneath the covers. She shut her eyes and knew herself turned toward sleep. It is almost four, she told her doubtful mind. Tomorrow I'm getting out of this cold dark place. At four o'clock the milkman and the paper boy come. At four o'clock the sun remembers us.

Images came and went behind her eyes. But none were strong enough to inhibit slumber. She fell, like Icarus, toward eternal morning. She went to sleep.

Chapter 6

Someone was building a scaffold. The sounds of the hammer blows were loud and blunt and frightening. Sara kept trying to tell them that no scaffold need be twelve stories high; but they kept on building it, adding plank after plank until it towered above an empty plain. The higher it grew the louder the hammering became until with a start she opened her eyes and saw sunlight on the floor and knew that someone was knocking at her door.

She rose hastily, snatching her robe from the foot of the bed, and crossed the rooms to the front door.

"Just a minute, please. Just a minute," she called querulously.

"Mrs. Hillstrom?" Mr. Bishop's drawl came through the door. "I'm real sorry if I waked you, but I rang up and rang up, and there wasn't no answer. I was beginning to wonder if maybe there was something wrong."

She squinted at her watch. Good heavens. It was eleven o'clock. She didn't know when she'd ever slept so late. She felt embarrassed and at a terrible disadvantage. "I'm sorry," she said.

"Well, no'm. I'm sorry," the voice came through the door. "But these fellows, they got here with your belongings and I didn't hardly know what to do about it. I figured you'd want them brought up."

She was confused and wished she had time to wash her face, but she slid back the chain and opened the door. Mr. Bishop stood stolidly with the two moving men behind him. They all three tipped caps at her, and she nodded and moved aside.

They came in, carrying the television set, and she pointed wordlessly at the spot by the fireplace where the cable came through the wall. They put the set down and went away for her boxes.

She felt completely disoriented. For a moment she was pleased that they'd arrived so promptly. Then she remembered that she wasn't going to stay here. She could hardly tell them to turn around and take the things back to the other place. She just stood, barefooted and disheveled in the middle of the floor, and let them walk around her.

"Just put the boxes anywhere," she said when they looked at her quizzically, and they stacked them side by side near the front door.

"Sorry to bother you," one of the movers said, handing her a slip to sign. "But we had this other load out this way and had to drop yours off."

"It's all right," she said, signing automatically, her freshly wakened mind trying to deal with the intricacies of moving it all back again later. She shrugged and showed them out the door, Mr. Bishop still apologizing, the two movers laughing and chaffing each other down the hallway to the elevator.

She shut the door and stood staring at her television set. If she had had it for company, the last two nights might not have been so bad, she thought. Now here it was after she'd already made the decision not to stay.

She went to put her coffee on and stubbed her toe on a kitchen chair. Tears of pain and anger came to her eyes, brought on as much by the thought of having overslept so badly as by the pain. She shook her head and had her coffee, trying to arrange her mind as though she hadn't lain slugabed, missing the morning hours.

She would take some clothes and the radio and the coffeepot back with her. She really didn't need anything else. She'd done without the TV here. She could certainly do without it in the old apartment. By the time she finished her second cup of coffee she was able to hum to herself as she got the things ready to go back with her.

At last she slammed her suitcase lid and stood uncertainly, wondering how she was going to get it all down to the car. She wasn't about to call Mr. Bishop and explain to him that she wasn't going to stay here. She couldn't face the thought of that. She picked up the box containing the coffee things and the radio and held it under one arm, picking up the suitcase with her other hand. She could manage if she stopped and set one of them down occasionally.

She looked around the apartment. There was absolutely nothing she wanted to do to it. She carried the things into the hall and locked the door behind her. They were heavier and more awkward to carry than she'd thought, but she managed to maneuver them into the elevator and back out at the other end.

This morning the parking space didn't seem half as formidable, even though her own car was still a lone and lonely object in its depths. She carried the things to it and put them in and turned the key in the ignition with a feeling of triumph.

As she drove down the ramp and out into the sunshine she could hear voices from the pool area and the sound of machinery. Oh dear, she thought. Nice Mr. Bishop is having that pool filled for me and I'm not going to be here. But it didn't dampen her mood. She drove out of the grounds and onto the highway with the feeling of a child escaping from school on the last day of term. Even the usually discourteous drivers seemed courteous this noonday. She drove, with no feeling of impediment, through the shopping circle, over the bridge where the water sparkled in midday delight, and to her own shaded street.

The gardener was weeding a flower bed, staying within the shade of an oak tree as much as possible. There seemed an unusual number of cars in the parking lot, but this, she knew, was probably just because she had grown so accustomed to the sight of her car sitting alone in the concrete cavern. She parked in the visitors parking area and went briskly toward Mr. Carter's cottage.

For a moment, as he came to the door, paper napkin in hand, she had a strong sense of *déjà vu*. Then she remembered that she had done this same thing only yesterday. It seemed much longer ago than that.

"Why, hello, Mrs. Hillstrom," Mr. Carter said. "Did them fellows get your things out there all right? They seemed a mighty light-minded couple of fellers to me. Joking and carrying on. Course, Lord knows, they're all that way nowadays. No sober-minded people left anywhere in the world, seems like."

"Mr. Carter," she said. "No. Yes. I mean they got it all there fine. It's just . . ."

"Forgot to leave both your keys, that it?" he said. "I noticed it yesterday. You left me one, but not the other."

"Well, that's just it." She smiled at him. "I won't be needing to turn it in at all. I'm going to move back."

A look of consternation crossed Mr. Carter's face. "Huh?" he said inelegantly.

"I want to move back. After all, I've paid up for the rest of this week. And I want to stay. I don't like it out there at all, Mr. Carter. This has gotten to be home to me. I want to stay here. I'm going to sell the apartment."

"Well, Mrs. Hillstrom." He looked embarrassed. He crumpled his paper napkin and looked down at it. "Of course, I realize that legally you got me about the rest of this week. And I could do something . . . but . . . Well, Jesus, Mrs. Hillstrom. The truth is I rented that apartment. I rented it yesterday right after you told me them boys would pick up the last of your stuff today. The folks are coming in tonight. Course, I *can* make arrangements. I can put them up in a motel at my own expense till your week's up. Guess that's what I deserve for being previous. But that's the best I can do, Mrs. Hillstrom. They want it for the whole summer, seems like. And I ain't got another thing. Ever one of my transient units are rented for at least a month ahead. Course, when one falls empty . . . Mrs. Hillstrom?"

It was terrible. The possibility of not being able to move back into the apartment hadn't even occurred to her. Not even in the loneliness of the condominium, not at the worst. She couldn't for a moment believe he could have said what he had. She stood frozen on his sunny doorstep, wanting to scream, to hit him, to make him disappear completely along with the words he'd said.

Because it was fate, the thing she'd been thinking about last night. This was simply the way it was. She could glean no consolation from his talk of an apartment falling empty by the end of the month. Nor any from the thought of spending the rest of the week here only to go back to the Triton when that week inevitably came to an end. She was lost. Whatever fate held for her in the confines of the Triton could happen in a month, or even in what was left of the month after a week of reprieve here. It made absolutely no difference in the long run. She was doomed to that place. After the initial thrill of horror, she realized that she'd known it all along.

"Mrs. Hillstrom," Mr. Carter was saying again. "Please. My God. Can't I help? Look, I'm sorry. We just got to work something out."

She realized then how her face must look. She knew she ought to say something, anything, but she couldn't. Instead she fumbled in her bag and handed him the remaining key, tied still to a thin brass ring, separate from her other keys. Then she turned and ran awkwardly to her car where, under the intermittent shadows of the oak tree, she gave in and cried the tears she hadn't let come until now.

Afterward she felt better. She blew her nose on a too-thin piece of tissue and dabbed ineffectually at her face. She sat for a moment before starting the car, taking stock. From where she sat she could see straight up into the boughs of the oak tree where a tiny bird was hopping busily from branch to branch, making a nest, no doubt. Hopefully a safe one, high enough to escape prowling cats, low enough to escape howling Gulf winds. She watched, bemused, feeling the sunlight on her face, talking to herself strictly, remembering talk of Howie's about overreaction, something he said her generation was always having. She supposed that was what she had just had. After all, Mr. Carter hadn't pronounced her death sentence. He'd merely said he'd rented the old apartment, and reality had to admit it was not all that much of an apartment.

Reality also had to admit that she shouldn't be thinking about trying to sell that condominium. If the building was empty now it was going to be a long time before it was filled, and why should anyone buy her apartment when the building was full of others which Mr. Snyder was no doubt pushing strongly.

It occurred to her that she had to depend on Mr. Snyder's salesmanship. She must hope he was a good salesman. Only he could bring her company in the night.

She started her car and drove away again from a part of her life. With almost a sense of gaiety she began to consider places for lunch. When you know the worst the only thing you can do is think about something else. She decided to browse the shopping center near the Triton. If that was where she was going to live, and it seemed it was, she might as well learn about the stores and restaurants nearest it.

She drove back across the bridge without looking at the water this time and found a parking space in a newly opened lot behind the power station. She walked around the block and into the circle. In the very center there was a small park and she crossed to it and sat on a stone bench. The sun was hot, but she knew that in a few moments she'd go somewhere cool for lunch and she wanted the moment to look at her surroundings. She wanted to tell herself that this busy crowded place was very near the empty Triton, and that during the night when she felt so alone and divorced from life, it was going on here.

On one side of the circle she could see a rock joint, proclaiming in large letters across the front that it was OPEN TILL. Which meant, of course, very very late. There were other bars too, though more discreet ones that might be expected to close their doors with midnight or one or two, that dreaded hour. There were several interesting restaurants, there were shops and delicatessens, and even an old-fashioned ice-cream parlor that made her nostalgic for a life that had disappeared completely somewhere along the way.

She chose a restaurant with care. From her vantage point she could see the people going into them and she chose the one where the people looked well-dressed and happy and festive. She wanted very much, if not to feel festive, at least to see someone who did.

It was cool inside the restaurant and crowded; it was evidently a popular place at lunch time. She and Howard had eaten here a time or two, but always at night. Restaurants at lunch are always a different place.

The maitre d' came toward her and asked if she had a reservation. When she shook her head he asked if she'd mind waiting in the bar for a few moments.

She did mind, but she followed him meekly. The bar was a pleasant place, but it was crowded too. She had to perch on a stool at the bar itself, something she always hated, and of course, she would have to buy a drink. She remembered the Bacardi and shuddered. The bartender was waiting and she thought of sherry, but remembering the sticky taste that had led her into that other apartment last night she knew she didn't want that. "Scotch and soda," she said bravely, and then sat nursing the glass and trying to look dignified perched precariously on the red leather stool.

She looked around the room, trying to discern the mood of the others in the bar. At a corner table two elegant girls were drinking champagne and eating steak sandwiches. They were both talking volubly, waving their hands for emphasis. Occasionally a word from one or the other of them would float up through the undercurrent of constant noise. The word generally seemed to be *He.*

At another table two old men in Bermuda shorts were buying drinks for two young girls in miniskirts. At another table two old women in miniskirts seemed to be buying drinks for two young men in Bermuda shorts.

A middle-aged couple drank beer and ate sausages in a dark corner.

Three young men in business suits were drinking martinis and arguing.

None of these people looked festive at all.

She sipped her Scotch and thought that it tasted scorched, a strange thing for whiskey. She cut her eyes toward her left and saw the elbow and back of an elderly gentleman. She cut her eyes to the right, and a bright young face smiled at her. She smiled back.

The girl looked very young, but who could tell any more. At any rate she was pretty, with blond hair, curls escaping from a topknot, and very blue eyes. "Hello," she said.

"Hello," Sara said back.

The girl was wearing a bright costume—what they called tie-dye, Sara thought. It was pink and green and gray, very lovely colors, and it seemed to consist of a vest and skirt. The vest met rather precariously over the girl's bosom and hooked with small frogs. She didn't seem to have anything on under it, though there was a long string of beads over it.

She reminded Sara of Ely and made her rather homesick for what was left of her family. For that reason she didn't turn away immediately but said, "That's an awfully pretty outfit you have on."

"Well, thanks," the girl said. "Just for that I'll stand the next round. Drink up."

"Oh, no thanks," Sara said, looking dubiously at her half-full glass.

"Oh sure," the girl said. "Come on. Drinking lunch is always fun. Even when you're alone, like you and I seem to be."

She made a motion toward the bartender and turned up her own glass. "This is the way it's done," she said, finishing the drink.

The bartender set two new ones in front of them.

The girl smiled. "You live here?" she said. "Or just visiting?"

"Oh, I live here," Sara said.

"Me too," the girl said. "At least for the present. My name's Sara."

"How very odd," Sara said, looking suspiciously at her Scotch. "Mine is too."

"How marvelous," the girl said. "I love things like that."

Sara smiled. The girl was so ingenuous, so fresh and childlike, in spite of the provocative clothes and the aura of worldliness. Maybe, she thought, all the young ones are really like that. They're children, but we've let ourselves be put off by the trappings, the things they wear, the things they say. She wanted suddenly to communicate with the girl beside her, understand something about her, maybe through her understand something about Howie and Ely and all the strange children she half feared.

She realized it was an odd thing to be thinking, but she'd thought so many odd thoughts during the last few days. One more couldn't make much difference.

The girl was chattering away beside her. "I love this bar," she was saying. "It's just dark enough and just light enough and it smells good and they're fast on the drink. It's about the only place in this town I do like. But I like it."

"You don't like Cape Haze?" Sara said.

"No. But that's probably unfair to Cape Haze. I've had a bad time here." She drank deeply and sighed. "I'm getting my second divorce," she said. "This is no place for a thing like that. This town is literally swamped with divorcees and widows. They tear

94

men to bits like the maenads. So what you have are gun-shy men and frantic ladies. I can't stand either." She looked at Sara. "You don't look frantic," she said.

You should have seen me a little while ago, Sara thought. Or last night.

"I'm a little past the age for that," she said.

The girl appraised her carefully. "Oh no you're not," she said.

But I want to be, Sara thought. I guess that's something. "Well, it can be a lonely town," she said.

The girl's eyes turned somber. "Oh yes," she said. "Yes indeedy. It can be that."

The next two hours became a hazy vagueness in Sara's mind, so that later, drinking coffee in the drugstore before grocery shopping, she wasn't sure it had all really happened the way she thought. The glasses of Scotch seemed to keep getting refilled at an alarming rate, and though she didn't feel at all tight everything seemed to assume unusual proportions. Words became portentous, thoughts seemed very clear and well defined. Everything had a sense of great rightness and understanding.

Eventually they moved to the table vacated by the two girls and had lunch, and during the salad and soup she learned a great deal about the small blond Sara across the table from her.

It seemed strange and perhaps sordid, but at the same time immensely interesting and just the thing she needed to hear today before going back alone to her tower.

Small Sara turned out to be not as young as she had thought. "I missed the mod scene and the hip culture," she said. "I was just too old to switch from alcohol to pot. Maybe it's just as well. I escalate everything so damned badly."

She had been born in a small town in the Midwest, to parents who were farmers. Life had been very simple and very dull in the plains, and at sixteen she'd moved into town and gotten a job in the ten-cents store after school in the afternoons. Her parents, who'd never seen the point in education for a girl, were so upset by the idea of her working in a dime store that they'd decided to send her to college.

She'd gone for two years to a small teacher's college, and there she'd found out that she could sing.

"Not really sing," she said. "Like opera. But I had what they call style. I'm still pretty good."

She'd gone to work after class with a small combo in a neighboring joint and she'd learned to enjoy a drink now and then and she'd fallen in love with the piano player and quit school and married him.

"As they say," she told Sara, "it was a bummer. All the way."

There was a lot of talk then about a life Sara couldn't even imagine; one-night stands, after-hours clubs and bar dates, a husband subject to the blandishments of female customers. A life lived on the fringe of big money when you had hardly any money at all.

"But when the marriage fell apart," the girl said, a certain slyness in her face, "I had learned a few things. I married somebody with a hell of a lot of money the second time." She laughed. "That's why I'm sitting out this divorce in sunny Cape Haze on the customer side of a nice bar."

She tilted her head at Sara and smiled that innocent smile. "The trouble is," she said, "I loved him. I didn't mean to. I meant to love all that money. But it didn't work out that way. I still love him," she added almost belligerently. "Ain't that a kick?"

Sara didn't know what to say to any of it. She nodded and tried to look sympathetic, and sipped her Scotch, and ate her lunch. The girl didn't seem to mind. She wanted to talk, and she did.

"But why didn't it work out?" Sara said finally after the girl's loving and somewhat drunken description of her second husband.

The girl stared at her, a small frown between her eyes. Then she shook her head. "Does it ever?" she said.

"Of course it does," Sara said automatically.

The girl just sat there, shaking her head. "Who are you kidding, lady?" she said finally.

Sara was so taken aback she felt quite sober again. "But it works out quite often," she said. "Doesn't it?"

The girl continued to shake her head.

"It did for me," Sara said.

"Did it?" the girl said.

Sara felt a sudden flash of anger. But she realized instantly that she had put herself in this ridiculous position. She should never have started drinking with a stranger in a bar. It was bound to get you into a situation. This was worse than being with Mary Appleby. She knew that she simply could not let this sort of thing start happening to her out of loneliness. She was going to have to get herself in hand. Take bridge lessons, join a club, something . . .

The girl was quiet now. "I'm sorry," she said suddenly. "I'm never much on tact. But it's true that the male-female relationship doesn't make it. You learn to enjoy what you can and put up with the rest. Or you don't. I don't. I can't. I've never learned to give in. I can't make that scene. Sure it works if you can do that."

The statement sounded so much like Moira that Sara felt reassured. This was just a girl like Moira after all who had made the mistake of getting married twice. She felt better about her then, and friendly toward her again. "This is on me," she said, reaching for the check.

"Certainly not," the girl said, taking it from her. "I've been telling you. Money is not anything I lack any more."

"Dutch, then," Sara said.

"You buy the lunch, I'll catch the bar," she countered.

"All right," Sara said, giving in, though she knew she was getting the best of it.

She would have liked to make the small friendly gesture of paying, but she saw that the girl didn't want it.

They went out of the dark bar into a brilliantly sunlit street.

Both of them reached for sunglasses and put them on, giving the world back a little of the darkness of the bar. Sara wanted only to go away quickly now, to drink coffee alone in the drugstore across the street, to make a shopping list and buy groceries. She still felt disoriented, but underneath was a firm resolve to start putting shape into her life by resigning herself to the way it was now going to have to be lived.

But the girl seemed reluctant to move away toward her own pursuits. She stood on the pavement, looking at Sara. "You haven't told me a thing about yourself," she said. "Come on now, that's not fair. I'm going to buy you a present for being so patient with me and I want you to tell me about you."

"There's nothing to tell," Sara said, laughing uneasily. "Nothing at all. I've lived a very normal uneventful life."

The girl laughed too. "Nobody lives that," she said, and the words seemed to carry a somber connotation. "Come on," she said. "The place I want to go is just across the street."

"I need to get home," Sara said.

"It won't take a minute," the young Sara said. "Honest. There's something I want to get for you. Come on."

Sara didn't know how to get out of it. She followed the bright creature across the hot pavement, feeling a puff of warm wind from the Gulf that blew a sudden cloud over the sun, dropping her into an instant depression. Aftermath of that Scotch, she thought. Well, there's nothing to do but go along with her. I can't be rude. After all, I started talking to her.

The girl seemed to twinkle across the street like a brilliant bird. She stopped on the other side and waited for Sara, laughing. "Come on, now," she said. "Right around the corner. And you still haven't said a word about yourself, have you? Except you did say it worked for you. Are you here with your husband?"

"He's dead," Sara said flatly.

"Oh, I'm sorry," the girl said. "I'm very sorry. Particularly as you think it worked. Do you live alone?"

"Yes," Sara said.

"I know," the girl said. "In one of those dreadful condominiums. Right?"

"Right," Sara said tersely.

"Which one?"

"The Triton," Sara said. She was beginning to feel annoyed, just as she had at Theodore Snyder with his questions. Why did people find it necessary to quiz you about things that were none of their business?

"Do many people live there?" the girl said.

"No," Sara said.

"I thought not," she said. "It must be awfully lonely. You must come over and see me sometime. I've got a wonderful beach cottage at the Midnight Beach, all paid for by Mr. Ex. At night I can even sit at the piano bar and not give a damn what the piano player's doing. Life has its compensations. Here we are."

They were standing in front of a record shop. Sara looked uneasily at the window filled with albums of rock groups and singers she knew nothing about.

"Come on," the girl said, and held the door open for her.

The interior was dark and dim again, like the bar. The narrow room was lined with bins in which records were filed as though in filing cabinets. A bored young man sat behind the cash register. He ignored them.

Young Sara flitted up and down the aisles, looking. Then she spied what she had evidently come for and turned her back to the particular bin, smiling at Sara. "I want to buy you a record," she said.

"But I don't have a . . ." Sara began, and stopped. It was true she didn't have a record player, but she had a feeling that it would make this happy-sounding girl very angry if she refused the present. She wasn't sure why she felt that way, something about the gleeful, almost secret stance of the girl in front of the records, something in the slightly imperious tone her voice had assumed since they'd left the bar.

Sara knew quite well that what she felt was fear, but she refused to countenance it. Still, she didn't finish the sentence. "A record?" she said.

"A record," the girl said. "But first I have to tell you my final secret. Being as you know all the rest." She laughed, a small, half-stifled trill, a very familiar laugh. "You see, I've become a Jesus freak," she said.

"A what?" Sara said.

The girl started to laugh again, then stopped and looked at Sara from behind the huge round panes of her sunglasses. "That means I dig Jesus," she said. "It's supposed to be a real new sort of thing. But the awful truth is—and how well I know all the awful truths—that it's really just my old Baptist inheritance coming back to save me from the devil. Isn't that truly awful? Truly, truly awful?"

Oh dear, Sara thought. The child isn't right. It isn't just drinking . . .

"No, dear Sara," the girl said, and now all trace of humor had faded from her voice. "I'm not crazy. I just face facts. I face the fact that what we once were always comes back to claim us, no matter how far we think we've escaped."

She turned away from Sara then as though completely uninterested in her. She picked up an album, went forward and paid for it, and thrust it into Sara's hand.

"There you are," she said briskly. "A little present from me to you. Listen to it. It's bound to do you good."

She walked rapidly to the door and through it and down the street without another word.

Sara stood staring down at the album in her hand. *Jesus Christ Superstar*. She looked at the clerk who was watching her, a smile on his face.

"What exactly is this record?" she said.

"It's a rock opera about Jesus," he said.

"Really about Jesus?" she said.

"Yes," he said. "Jesus of Nazareth. That's the one *you* mean, isn't it?"

"Thank you," she said, and hurried away from his insolent gaze.

The drugstore was only a few doors away and she hurried toward it, glancing up and down the street as she went. But bright-plumaged Sara had vanished.

She went inside and sat on a low stool at the counter—which suited her far better than a high bar stool—and drank coffee and tried to compose her mind.

The whole incident had been so atypical there was nothing she could compare or anchor it to. The girl had seemed so bright and amusing and pleasant, a reminder of youth and all the good things. She had changed in the telling of her story, but had remained essentially bright, essentially young and appealing. It was only in the record shop that something had happened, that the vaguely threatening thing had seemed to emanate from her.

Sara wondered if she had imagined the whole thing. Because, she told herself, I am becoming imaginative. It has to do with being alone. I am going to call Mary Appleby tonight, or one of the bridge clubs. I can't go on sitting around thinking peculiar things.

But the girl *had* been peculiar. There was no point in trying to blame that on herself. She was a real girl with real problems and those problems had made her that way. But it needn't concern her. Not in any important way.

She looked down at the album on her lap. She supposed she could play it in the community room of the condominium. She'd have to ask Mr. Bishop.

It was only then, thinking of his fat, placid face, that she remembered the TV cable people were supposed to come. She went to a phone booth in the back of the store and called Mr. Bishop.

"Oh, they've already come, Mrs. Hillstrom," he said, sounding his usual sane self. "I let them in. I didn't think you'd mind. They're so hard to get hold of, figured you'd want it done while they were here."

"Yes, thank you," she said. "It'll be nice to have it."

"I stayed there with them the whole time," he said. "It was all right."

"I'm sure it was," she said. "Oh, Mr. Bishop. Is there a phonograph in the community room?"

"Yes mam," he said. "Real good one, 3 speed. And some records, though not as many as should be. We're kinda low on books too, but there are some. By the way, the pool's filled."

"That's very nice," she said politely. "I'll see you later."

"Yes mam," he said. And rang off.

She sat in the booth for a moment, holding a humming receiver. Everything had been prepared for her at the Triton. The TV was in, the pool was filled, there were records and books in the community room. She wondered why she had ever supposed that she could escape. She sighed, put the receiver down, and went back for more coffee which she drank while making out a neat grocery list on the back of an envelope.

The grocery store on the circle was half supermarket, half delicatessen. She wandered happily around it, sniffing the odors of cheese and pickles, cold meats, coffee, iced shrimp, raw meat.

What she wanted to do was buy exotic things, small jars of caviar, snails with their shells neatly canned in a separate container, blue cheese, jellied consommé. She didn't. She propped her gift record in the cart and went methodically about buying half of what she usually bought for any ordinary week. Bacon and eggs and bread, oleo and coffee, vegetables and fruit, lamb chops, hamburger, steak.

She did treat herself to some exotic tea and some English muffins, and, at the last minute, a little bag of licorice. She loved licorice, but she knew it was a juvenile and silly craving, and generally she was able to ignore it. Today she thought, Why not? There was so little in her life. It couldn't hurt.

She realized at the checkout counter that there were no magazines in this particular store and that she'd have to go back to the drugstore. But the size of her grocery sack and the awkward bulk of the record album discouraged her, and she walked on to her car instead. After all, she could read one of those "few books" in the condominium library.

She put the things down beside the car, unlocked it, and looked in consternation at the suitcase and box in the back seat. The events of the afternoon had almost made her forget her flight and the refusal of sanctuary. It came back to her now in all its sadness, but at least it was just that, sadness, and resignation. It wasn't, at least not yet, fear. The only fear she'd felt this afternoon had concerned the strange little girl in the record shop. And that fear was out in the sunlit streets of Cape Haze; not lurking in her apartment.

I will have the TV tonight, she thought, stowing in the groceries and the album. And for late afternoon, of course, the pool. Maybe sitting on the edge of the pool will give me another perspective about the Triton.

But the Triton, when it loomed before her, seemed no more welcoming than before. She went to her parking space and began the long process of getting everything out of the car, through the swinging door, and up in the elevator. It took three trips because none of the objects could be handled with one hand except the suitcase. Even the record album was a problem, due to its shape.

Finally all the things stood lined up outside her door and she opened it and took them in.

The television stared cheerfully at her from the corner, and after locking the door, she went to it and turned it on. They had adjusted it nicely for her, and she looked with approval at Walter Cronkite, life size and in color, telling her all the terrible news in a voice that somehow kept it all from being so terrible. She appreciated that in Walter Cronkite. Brinkley had always made her feel stupid; Huntley, somehow weary. And in the long ago days of Gabriel Heatter . . . well . . . he had always foreseen doom so inevitably that she could never stand to listen to him at all.

She left Walter speaking in the living room and went to put away her groceries. That, too, was a cheerful act. It was the first time her refrigerator had looked used. She unpacked her cardboard box again and put it back beside the garbage can.

Then she remembered the pool and went outside to stand on the balcony and peer over the edge at the oblong of concrete below. It was full now, the water still and blue in the late afternoon. Someone—Bishop or Snyder, no doubt—had set out a table with a beach umbrella and several chairs. She stood looking down into the water, feeling almost festive. After all, she thought, it is my own private pool, just waiting for me to lounge around it like someone in an advertisement. Tomorrow I might even think about getting a sun tan.

She felt very determined to feel and act in a normal fashion. After all, she knew now the impossibility of escape. When one's course of action was certain and unalterable one made the best of it.

She went in and went about preparing her supper with efficient movements. It gave her a certain sadness to fix only one chop, but she tried not to dwell on that fact either. The liquor of lunch time had worn off completely and it occurred to her that it might be fun to fix herself a before-dinner cocktail and have it while she cooked. She went to the living room and rummaged in the box of household things. There was a lot of Scotch in the bottle because neither she nor Howard ever drank Scotch, but, looking at it, she remembered vividly Sara in the noontime bar and had no appetite for it. She set the bottle on her kitchen counter and had a cigarette instead.

It occurred to her that she hadn't even thought of a cigarette all the time she'd been out today, not even when Mr. Carter had turned her away from the old apartment. Smoking cigarettes must be a thing I do only in the Triton, she thought. It must be a form of company. Like Walter Cronkite on the television screen.

By the time her supper was ready Walter had gone away and she had to watch a rather silly situation comedy while she ate on a TV table in the living room. But that was company too.

Still briskly, she washed up and went to the telephone to make a call to Mary Appleby. You see, she told herself, finding the number with no trouble, and dialing. It is all a frame of mind. Everything seemed normal and even, she was happy to note, a little dull.

Mary Appleby wasn't in. Well, of course she wouldn't be, Sara thought. It's the time of night when everyone is out for dinner. I'll have to call her at a reasonable time. She tried to think of when that might be and failed utterly. Morning wouldn't do, of course. She knew Mary must sleep late. Noon was lunch time. Maybe between three and five. What strange lives people lead nowadays, she thought. They can only be reached at home between three and five.

She tried all the stations on the television, but nothing looked interesting to her. I'll have to get a *TV Guide* tomorrow when I get my magazines, she thought.

She sat in the big blue chair and watched another situation comedy. Dark was falling outside and she went to the window to see the round globes of light come on below her. They lit up the pool as bright as day. She could even swim at night, she thought. If she were someone else. She couldn't see herself going all the way downstairs in a bathing suit or coming all the way up again afterward. The swimming itself might be all right. Out there in the lights and open air. But she knew she wouldn't do it.

The record album was still propped against her suitcase beside the front door. She sat looking at it for a while. If she had a phonograph she could play it now. Perhaps it was something soothing, a religious record, even with that outlandish title. At least it was about something religious. But they hadn't had a phonograph since Howie had gone away. He had always had one and when he was in the house it had been on, too, playing everything from classical music to this rock stuff. But she had never listened to any of it. It was a part of the background noise, sounds emanating from Howie's room—nothing else.

There had just never been much music in her life.

She turned off the television and was shocked at the silence when its electronic voice died. She watched the small bright spot shrink to the middle of the screen and vanish. She lit another cigarette.

Well, she told herself, blowing blue smoke before her, the sensible thing to do, as you are going to be sensible, is go downstairs to the community room and play this on the phonograph there. Afterward you can pick up a book to read, and then perhaps it will be late enough for something good to be on television.

She liked the sound of the plan. It had such a nice solid filling-up-the-evening feel to it. That was the way other people who had to live alone behaved.

But first she wanted to leave her apartment to come back to. She unpacked the suitcase, putting all the clothes back into the closet and drawers. She turned down her bed and turned on her bed lamp. She even put fresh cigarettes in a box on both the TV set and her bedside table.

She picked up her purse and the record album and went to the door. Just as she put her hand on the knob she remembered the balcony door and went back and locked it, a small flutter of fear starting in her chest, which she repulsed by thinking of how far it was from the ground to this floor.

Outside her door, still carried along by her own plans and resolutions, she turned to the left before going to the elevator and went to the door of the apartment next door. It was still standing lightly ajar and with a firm hand she pulled it closed and heard the satisfying click as the latch caught. She tried the door and saw that it had automatically locked. She nodded, pleased, and went down the hall to the elevator.

Mr. Bishop, his back to her, was talking on the telephone in the lobby. She could hear his voice between long pauses. "Huh? Yeah. I don't know."

She smiled, and tried to make some sort of noise as she approached him so that he wouldn't be startled, but the carpet deadened all sound. Just as she reached the desk she heard him say, "Well, I don't know. I think she's jumpy enough as it is."

The words sent a chill to Sara's heart. Was he talking about her? And to whom? Nonsense. He could be talking about anybody to anybody. Probably his wife, or one of his children. She walked on around the desk.

Mr. Bishop was startled after all. He nodded at her, but a dull red suffused his face. "I got to go now," he said hastily into the phone, and hung up.

He's pretty jumpy himself, Sara thought. "Thank you for getting my TV in," she said.

"Welcome," he said. "They get it working O.K.?"

"It's fine. But nothing's on right now. I thought I'd go into the community room and try that phonograph." She held up the record album as though it were a passport.

"Sure," he said. "Come along and I'll turn things on for you."

She followed him down the hall and through a wide archway into a very large room. There was only one dim light burning over the mantelpiece, but he quickly flicked switches and flooded the empty spaces. "The phonograph's right over here," he said. "Let me see if it's plugged up."

She walked over to the windows and looked out. The view was of the lighted pool and beyond it, the ocean. The pool looked clear and smooth and blue under the lights. Then suddenly she saw something break the surface of the water, a sleek round thing like a seal. She stood there staring at it for long seconds before she realized that it was someone's head.

"Why Mr. Bishop," she said. "There's someone in the swimming pool."

Chapter 7

Behind her Mr. Bishop knocked over a lamp. She could hear the sudden crash and then the small tinkling going on and on as the glass bulb shattered and she realized he must have dropped it onto the hearth.

She knew all this below the threshold of instant panic caused by the sound, but for a frozen moment she couldn't turn and look to verify it. Then she did and saw Mr. Bishop, red-faced, making ineffectual noises at the mess on the floor. She looked quickly back at the pool. There was nothing there at all. Except the calm blue water of before. She kept looking, but nothing broke the surface again.

"What did you say, Mrs. Hillstrom?" Mr. Bishop finally said behind her.

"I saw someone in the pool," she said, thinking how inane the words sounded after the noise and confusion of the smashing glass.

"I don't reckon you did," Mr. Bishop said more calmly. "Couldn't be nobody out there. I just come in from a look around the grounds."

"But I saw them," she said reasonably, trying to keep her voice level. How ridiculous of the man to argue with her just because he'd broken a lamp.

He came to her side and looked out the window. "I don't see anybody," he said.

"I don't either . . . now," Sara said. "But there was someone."

He gave her a patronizing look. "All right," he said, sighing heavily. "I'll go out and look. I'd hate for some of them kids around here to get the idea that pool was for public use. But I think you must have been mistaken."

She looked at him sternly, feeling for the first time her proper relationship to him. His clumsy breaking of the lamp had reminded her that he was the servant, she the mistress.

"I'm going," he said. "Then I'll come back and clean up that mess."

After he left she still stood at the window, watching the empty pool. In a few moments she saw him come around the corner of the building, looking left and right. He went up to the edge of the pool and looked into its depths, he turned around and shrugged at her. He walked down toward the beach and looked up and down the sand, shining a flashlight in front of him. Then he came back, walking clumsily, and she could see the light dancing around the corner of the building and up toward the palm trees.

She kept watching the pool until she heard him coming back inside the building.

"Nobody nowhere," he said. "Must have been a leaf."

There was something in his voice that Sara couldn't place. She listened to it and to the echo of it in her mind. Why, he was lying. She knew exactly that tone and sound. It was the way any man who couldn't lie always sounded, just a tiny bit too sincere. She'd heard Howard do it, and Howie. She turned and looked at him.

He was sweeping up the mess made by the lamp. The lamp itself stood tipsily on the edge of the hearth, the socket dislocated, the cord dangling crookedly. The shade was crumpled and punctured by glass bits. Mr. Bishop leaned over his dustpan with a short-handled broom. He didn't look up.

She didn't know what to say to him. There wasn't anything to say. There didn't seem to be any reason for him to lie. But he was lying. She knew that quite well. She continued to watch him sweeping up the mess. She was very glad that she hadn't buzzed down for him on either of the nights before. She could see him, shining that flashlight around the empty apartment next to her and saying, "Nobody there at all." And what if she had listened to his voice then and heard that same over-sincerity. She didn't like to think about that.

He stood up from the hearth, but he still didn't meet her eyes. "Well, better get this out," he said. "The phonograph's all right."

"Thank you," she said.

He went out the door.

She looked back at the swimming pool, peaceful under the lights. She looked around the room. She was here now. She might as well follow her plan and play the record and select some books. She walked across the room to the phonograph. The books and records—and Mr. Bishop had been right, there were pitifully few of them—were in shelves over the phonograph and TV set. There were several armchairs pulled up around the area and she sat in one and unwrapped the album. Then she put the record on the spindle and looked up at the books. There really wasn't anything there that she wanted to read, but she selected two novels, carefully avoiding the several mysteries in bright covers. That's all I need, she told herself grimly. And remembered reading *Miss Pinkerton* years ago when she was still at home and all the family had been asleep. She'd been so frightened she'd had to get a pillow and lie on the floor outside her parents' door to go to sleep.

She turned on the phonograph and watched the record drop into place before going back to the chair she'd selected because it faced both the pool and the archway into the room.

When the music began it confused her so much she couldn't make head nor tail of it. It was merely sound, just as the music from Howie's room had always been. She realized she had the volume turned up too high and went over and turned it down. At least now she could distinguish between the music and words. She set the record back to the start.

Then she looked down at the album and realized the words were there, printed on a small folder. It was easier for her then. She could at least follow them, know who was speaking, understand that this *was* Jesus of Nazareth, and the disciples, and Mary Magdalene, even if the words they were saying in the strange voices of today seemed to have no connection with them.

The record played and finished and the second one dropped, and she began to realize that she was fascinated with the whole thing; that the young voices speaking raucously and incomprehensively were more real to her than anything she'd ever heard about Jesus in that stuffy old Sunday-school room of childhood. She couldn't approve of Jesus sounding like a hippie, nor Magdalene like a clear-eyed teen-ager, but she had to admit it was very real. For a time she forgot she was supposed to be watching a lighted pool and an empty archway and followed the words to the strange music almost as though she were at home.

What a strange present for that strange girl to give me, she thought, as the second record came to an end and she sat still for a moment before rising to turn them over.

If Howie had given this to her she could have understood it. He would have been trying to educate her and ribbing her a little at the same time. But that wasn't why that girl had done it. It was as though she had known it would interest her. Howie wouldn't have thought that at all. Howie—like Howard, like Mr. Bishop, like all the men she had ever known—patronized her. While blond Sara had had that note of menace and meanness in her voice there at the end, it hadn't been patronizing. Oh no, it had been rather as though she had known something about Sara that Sara didn't know herself.

Don't start that, she thought, and got up to turn over the records. It was just at the moment when the needle dropped onto the record and she prepared to start reading the second half of the opera that she remembered the girl's laugh. It came to her, bright and vivid above the sound of the record; and she knew, quite simply and finally, where she'd heard it before. It was the same laugh she'd heard in the emptiness of her apartment. There wasn't any doubt about it. It was, in intonation, timbre, quality, exactly the same.

But what does it mean? she thought, staring again out the window until the globed lights blurred to her vision. What can that possibly mean? Surely it doesn't mean anything. I simply won't think about that.

She went back to the phonograph and firmly started the record over and sat down, gluing her eyes to the printed words before her, tuning in again the strange music of a stranger Galilee.

Sara was not a religious woman. She would have said she was if anyone had asked her, but it was lip service and a part of her knew this. She didn't feel strongly about religion any more than she did about most things. I'm just not a woman of strong feelings, she often said. She thought now of herself saying this and she wondered with that new inner voice if she'd been saving it all up for this time of loneliness in the Triton tower. Certainly she'd felt enough in the last few days to last her a lifetime, before and after. And now she was feeling religious while listening to those raucous sounds of the younger generation. She wondered if she might need some vitamins or maybe a liver shot.

For, again, the strange power of the record was taking her mind away from the immediate surroundings, making her forget Mr. Bishop and someone in the swimming pool and a stifled laugh. Well, so much to the good.

Then the record changed and the Crucifixion began.

Sara listened in a state of shock. The whole depiction was so real she felt as though she were standing on Golgotha; and when the hammer blows began she knew that the sound was a sound she had heard, not just this morning in her interrupted dream, but somewhere in the dim recesses of her mind through all her life.

She listened through to the end and sat quite still in her chair in the empty room, listening to the echoes in her mind.

She felt strangely at peace and, at the same time, very sad. What a very very good thing that is, she thought in surprise. It is almost as real as the real thing must have been. Now why is it the church doesn't do that for us any more? I guess I'm at an age when I need the church to do a thing like that for me. And it just doesn't. How very strange that little girl should know this and give me this record. And why was she menacing about it? I simply don't understand anything at all tonight. Not anything at all.

She looked across the room at the abused lamp on the hearth corner. Certainly she hadn't imagined that. Mr. Bishop had broken a lamp when she had mentioned seeing someone in the pool, and then he had lied to her about it. That had happened. Blond Sara had obviously happened too. For here on the turntable was the record to prove her. Everything simply wasn't all in her mind.

She stood up and put her records back in the album and went across the long empty room to the hallway and out into the entryway. Mr. Bishop was nowhere in sight, but it neither surprised her nor frightened her. Whatever strange thing he might be up to was only a part of all the other strangenesses of today.

She went to the elevator and back to her room, happy that she'd left it habitable.

Once inside with the television on and the lights burning, she felt a great sense of satisfaction. There, she said to herself. I have spent the evening in the community room. I have listened to a record and selected books for reading. I have conversed with Mr. Bishop and come back to my cozy room.

And, her mind went on, You have seen a strange person in your swimming pool, and listened to a gift record about the death of God. And you're still scared.

No I'm not, she said, and watched a TV comic imitating his mother.

After a while she began to be aware that something was wrong in the room. Not a big thing, not an open door, a hidden presence, a thing to fear; but something small, minute even; something out of place or in the wrong place, something that wasn't the way it had been before.

She sighed, stood up, and began to look around the room. The furniture was in place, even the cushions on the couch were just as they had been when she left the room that noontime for the haven of the old apartment. She had straightened up any disorder she'd made moving back in. She'd even put the record album carefully away with her photograph book just now. The only new thing in the room was the chattering TV set and the two books, one of which she held, still unopened, on her lap.

But something was wrong. Finally she walked across the room and looked at her crystal collection. That was it, of course. The mouse was gone.

She stood for a long moment, staring at the space where he should have been. Not only was he gone, but the pieces that had flanked him on each side had been moved ever so slightly inward so that there was not even an empty space where he had been.

This is real, she told herself. This is even more real than Sara with the record or the head in the swimming pool. Much more real than a laugh or a clinking glass.

She began to look slowly along the shelves, searching out each piece, going over each piece in her mind, the when and where of acquiring it, the reasons for acquiring it, the solidness of each piece in her hand when she had first picked it up before purchase. Everything else was there. The mouse was not. She began moving each piece forward and looking behind it. But it wasn't there, and in a sudden panic she began taking each piece and setting it on the floor until she was ringed around by the delicate shining pieces, standing carefully and silently in the middle of them looking at an undeniably empty row of shelves. The mouse had simply disappeared.

Behind her there was a station break and a terribly nasal female voice began talking about her detergent. She felt defeated. Beaten. Incapable of thought or movement, even the desire to escape.

Life had become impossible. Not frightening any more, nor inexplicable. Just impossible.

She thought momentarily of kicking out at the crystal ringed around her feet and knew that even in a moment of impossibility she was incapable of such destruction. It was not a thought that comforted her at all.

She felt that she had been brought here, a victim to some unknown sacrifice and that it was to be performed bit by bit in small segments, a slicing off here, a burning off there. Taking the mouse was simply the first of the mutilations that lay in wait for her.

With a resignation quite beyond despair she leaned over and began picking up the crystal and putting it carefully back on the shelves the way it had been before.

Only she left the space where the crystal mouse had been. Let them see and know that she understood.

When all the crystal was back in place she turned and went back to her chair by the television set. The voices spoke of soap and stomach remedies and then it was time for the movie.

In spite of herself she felt a moment of anticipation because old movies were the one thing she really enjoyed on TV. Howard had always made fun of her choices which ran, she knew, to love stories, the love stories of a simpler time when love was a thing in itself, neither sex nor a reaching out to strangers in a foreign country. Love, for two people only, in a world prepared for and because of them and the shining thing that happened between them.

She knew the stories were old-fashioned and naïve and unrealistic. Certainly she knew that. It was—what did they call it?—campy to watch them. But she did watch them and she knew it wasn't for camp. It was because a part of her longed for that simpler world and for a few hours, sometimes, between the shrill-voiced ads, she had it.

Tonight, as though balancing out the loss of the mouse, they gave her Leslie Howard. She hadn't thought to ever see a Leslie Howard movie again.

She had always liked him, and Howard had always called him a pantywaist. Well, both of them were dead. Howard and Leslie Howard, and here she was watching an old Leslie Howard movie and remembering how it had been to be young and to dream. Perhaps whatever was going to happen to her was going to happen here, in front of the television set while the aesthetic face on the screen mouthed noble platitudes. She would watch him and ignore the cold place in her back and let whatever was going to happen happen.

But nothing did. Not through the three reels of what was really a very short movie, but which went on for a very long time because the station used the old movie time to catch up on all the ads they'd missed during the day.

Then it was over. Leslie Howard walked through the door back into his old life in black and white and it was The End. The ads came on in color. Love was in black and white. An oily-voiced pitchman was selling religious records aided by strange allies: a Korean choir, a man who looked like a used-car dealer, a couple who even Sara thought looked as though they did strange things to one another. She left them to sing "In the Garden" and went back to the shelves. The mouse was truly gone.

She had known that, of course, all the time she had been watching Leslie Howard, but she had pushed it to the back of her mind. Now the enormity of the empty space he left was in the room with her and she didn't know how to cope with it.

She made her mind work, rustily but coherently. She told herself in the syllables of a primer, You must look for it.

There were very few places in this new and clean and unlived-in apartment to look, but she looked in all of them.

In the empty fireplace, behind the golf trophies, under the couch. She opened the balcony door and looked under all the iron furniture in that cramped space. The bedroom was more difficult because there were more of her things there; but there was no crystal mouse. Nor in the bathroom, though she moved all the articles in the medicine cabinet out and lined them up neatly on the laundry hamper and then put them back. She even looked in all the half-empty kitchen cabinets and under the sink. That left the closets, and she couldn't face them yet.

It was all nonsense anyway. Why should anybody hide a crystal mouse? But then why should anybody take one? The shelves were full of much more valuable and more beautiful pieces of glass. Why take just that one? Except that, perhaps, it was the smallest, the one least likely to be missed.

At any rate a thief might reason that way. Anyone who knew Sara, anyone bent on torture for Sara, would know better; would know the mouse was the most important of all the pieces, know he was the key and reason for the whole collection.

She had not been really afraid since she'd discovered the disappearance of the mouse, not with the terror of the previous two nights. There had been no room for terror in the midst of loss and resignation. It was as though she had been given a sign. And, as with the discovery she could not move back to her old apartment, it was too enormous a discovery to elicit simple terror. Sounds from empty apartments, strange heads in swimming pools, disembodied laughs: those were the precursors of terror. Deliberate malevolence put the whole thing beyond terror, gave it the shape of inevitability she'd been approaching all day.

She sat down on a kitchen chair and thought about the events of the day, leading so inexorably from terror to resignation. Awaking to the knocking that continued from dream to reality with no crossing over between, standing in the sunlight and shade of the old apartment, hearing the words that condemned her to this tower, squinting in the sunlight while that strange child, Sara, made her a stranger gift, watching the dark shape in the pool

117

while behind her Mr. Bishop carelessly broke a lamp on the hearth of the community room.

Is it all in my mind? she thought. All of it? But it couldn't be. There was the record, and the broken lamp, and the missing mouse. Tangible objects connecting all the events. Except that the mouse seemed to be totally gone. Could it be that there simply never had been a mouse at all?

But *of course* there had been a mouse. Just thinking about it, she could feel the cold of that winter day as she stood in front of Dayton's, see the black velvet of the cloth on which he'd sat in the window, feel her own chapped hands inside her gloves, the unaccustomed weight and warmth of the fur coat that seemed to her a burden and a cheat.

She had never really longed for a fur coat, not in the way most of the women she knew did. Even Moira, even she, had wanted that symbol of female importance. Wanted it enough to buy it for herself. She'd been very proud of having bought it for herself. *My* mink, she'd said of it. Truly mine. I bartered nothing for it. Nothing at all. But Sara had thought then, and thought now, that if it hadn't meant anything to her as that symbol of female desirability, why had she wanted one at all?

"Because it is as cold as a witch's tit in Minneapolis," Moira had said. But that wasn't really the reason. It never was.

Sara hadn't wanted a fur coat, and Minneapolis was cold to her too. If she'd wanted one at all it would have been a beaver coat, shiny, smooth, warm, and practical. Mink meant nothing, meant less than nothing. Howard had given it to her because he'd been away.

Howard gave it to me because he'd been up to something, she said to her empty room. There are only two reasons for mink coats. Because *you* have or because *they* have. Either way is ugly. And I never wanted one.

I never wanted one and now I live in Florida where one is completely impractical and it is filed away at Kramer's department store in the deep freeze. If it had been here maybe they would have taken it and left me the mouse. That would have been much better. The mouse I wanted. Then and now. And I did have it. And it is gone.

The late news came on the television, reminding her that time had passed. At least the feeling of resignation was doing that for her. It had speeded up recalcitrant time, turned it into an ally. It was twelve o'clock. Four more hours until the beginning of morning. Only four more hours until another day.

With the thought and the glance at her watch, she knew she hadn't really disposed of terror at all. She was still Sara, alone in a tower meant for sixty-five families, still Sara, beleaguered by all the things that could be, had been, and were.

I didn't look in the boxes, she thought. Reluctantly she made herself rise and go slowly through them, the old ones that had been in the apartment from the beginning, the new ones brought in—when? Only yesterday? No. Only this morning. A million ticking seconds ago, centuries of time away. There was nothing in any of them that resembled a crystal mouse.

She became aware of silence and realized the TV station had gone off the air. Looking over her shoulder she saw the strange and fateful shape of the test pattern, fixed, immutable, on the face of the screen. She hurried across the room and turned the channel, but all of them had gone off. There was no late, late, movie tonight. She turned the set off.

The quiet seemed to gather after so long a time of the shadow-faces mouthing words into her life. She went to the bedroom and turned on her reliable all-night disc jockey with his country-western records and his truck-stop ads and his cheerful reminiscences about the great and near-great of the "Grand Ole Opry."

There was a part of her that had begun to enjoy this music, always before thought of as dissonant and irritating, nasal and shrill. Here, in loneliness, where it had become a source of humanity in the night, she realized she was listening to it, even waiting for certain records that she had heard before and was

119

beginning to enjoy. There was one in particular that seemed to have been written just for her at this moment in her life. "Help Me Make It Through the Night." Although the song had sexual overtones it was essentially a song about loneliness. It was a song she could understand. Now.

She thought that this turn of events would amuse both Howard and Howie, who knew so well her hatred of what she called hillbilly music. She didn't know which would amuse them the most, her liking for the rock opera or for this lonely country sound.

What else have I missed? she thought, hearing a voice telling her that it had been "A Good Year for the Roses." And why have They waited until it is far too late to start giving it to me?

Because it was too late. Something irrevocable was happening with the sureness of the sound of hammer blows, something that wasn't going to allow her long to listen to the different music of these days of her life. The mouse had gone. Who knew what would follow? It no longer even mattered whether she was here or somewhere else. She had inadvertently opened the door to the tower room and seen the heads on the wall. There was never any saving yourself after that.

She felt that this was the message pretty blond Sara had been trying to give her, and suddenly she wanted to call her. She knew that she was at the Midnight Beach, and she remembered the name of that second husband with the charm and money. Byer. Her name was Sara Byer.

She went to the telephone and found the number for the Midnight Beach. She dialed it and while she waited for the answer, looked at her watch. One o'clock. But that wouldn't matter. There was sure to be an all-night operator and Sara was certainly not an early-to-bed girl.

"Midnight Beach," a cheerful voice said.

"Could you connect me with Sara Byer's cottage?" she said.

"Just a moment," the voice said. There was a pause, then, "Could you repeat the name, please?"

She repeated it.

"I'm sorry. There doesn't seem to be anyone registered here by that name."

"There must be," Sara said. "Could you check again?"

"I just did," the voice said. "I checked for the last two weeks. There hasn't been anybody by that name."

"Oh," Sara said. "Well. Could you connect me with a phone near the piano bar?"

"They just closed up for the night. I saw Lew go out . . . the piano player. Sorry."

"Well. Thank you," Sara said. She tried to think of something else to say to keep the cheerful voice on the line, but there wasn't anything. "Thank you," she said again. After a moment there was only the empty humming of the wire. She put the phone carefully back in the cradle.

It didn't mean anything. The girl had probably been lying, saying she was staying at a good address when she was really in a dingy motel somewhere. Or she might even be there, but under another name, her maiden name, or that of her first husband, or a brand-new one, picked for the occasion. There were any number of explanations. It certainly needn't mean that there was no Sara. That, like the crystal mouse, she had disappeared. There was the record. She went to where she had put it. It was there.

But you could have bought that record yourself, the voice in her head said.

But I didn't, she said back.

She knew quite well that sometime during the day she had begun to walk a thin line between reality and unreality and that she had to do something about it. It had started because she had overslept. She knew this to be a simple characteristic of herself and not frightening, not unusual. If she slept too long, dreams lasted over into the day, it was too soon noon and she not rid yet of the night. The other events of the day had simply piled up on this original fact and coupled with her loneliness made her vulnerable to fantasy. The two previous nights of terror had taken their toll too. But now she knew she had to begin to reverse the process.

The best and simplest thing would be to sleep. But sleep before the promise of dawn was no longer a possibility. There were some pills in the medicine cabinet, prescribed for her after the doctor had discovered the heart scar, but never used. She had an innate fear of sleeping pills, and she knew that now they would be the worst thing possible for her. Sleep they might give her, or loss of consciousness, but not the sleep to restore health and perspective. They would only condemn her to another day of waking wrongly. She needed the sleep that comes from a glad tiredness. That kind of sleep was unpurchasable. She didn't have the coin.

She considered a drink and knew that to be wrong too. She thought of coffee and knew she didn't need the nervous edge. She fell back again on tea, willing herself to perform the movements of heating water, setting the tray, pouring into the pretty cup. She sat with her back to the kitchen wall, too tired to carry it into the living room, and warmed her hands on the cup as though the world were cold.

After a cup or two she remembered cigarettes and lit one, glad again for the gift of tobacco smoke. It drifted on the kitchen air and from the bedroom country music drifted with its sound of normalcy.

Pretend, Sara, she told herself. Pretend that this is just an ordinary day. That Howard is out at the club and will be in in a little while, that Howie is still at school and has just called home for money, that Moira is coming over tomorrow to talk. That you have cleaned up after supper and are getting ready for bed. If it were like that, miraculously, what would you make of all the events of this long and terrible day?

You would say that you had got up on the wrong side of the bed. That would account, right there, for most of it. You would say that you'd had too much unaccustomed liquor at lunch, and that would account for more. When Howard came in he'd reduce the head in the pool to a beach urchin illegally having fun; he'd reduce Sara to an alcoholic tramp; he'd turn Mr. Bishop into a bumbling idiot; he'd say the TV men had stolen your crystal mouse.

Of course. There had been somebody in the apartment. They'd simply taken the mouse away in their coverall pocket. In spite of Mr. Bishop's assertions that he'd been watching them all the time. After all, Mr. Bishop hadn't seen anything in the pool. And there had been something there. But she'd been sure there had been someone in that apartment next door last night too. And there hadn't been. She'd proved that to herself.

"I won't cry," she said. And poured more tea. "I will not cry."

But she had begun to listen again. It was two-thirty. Still an impossible time of night. I haven't looked in the closets, she told herself. I still haven't been able to look in the closets. *And I don't want to.*

She remembered suddenly, vividly, the voice of a long-ago boy cousin, come to visit for the summer: *Sara's a fraidy cat. Sara's a fraidy cat. She's a fraidy cat cause she's a girl.* And he had locked her in the corncrib and gone away.

She had sat there, watching dark come through a crack on the wall, so high up she knew she couldn't climb to it, having to go to the bathroom, afraid she'd give in and go to the bathroom, and holding onto that fact because it was better to fear that than the fact that they might not come there to look for her and she'd have to spend the night there alone in the dark.

With the thought she had the feeling that none of her life since then had been real. That she had been waiting, crouched in that corncrib, and that all the years with Howard, with Howie, with the miracles of modern appliances, with the fur coat and the ruby bracelet, and the cars and houses and boats had been nothing, a wink of the eye, an illusion leading to now where she was still just Sara, a fraidy cat locked in a corncrib with night coming on.

Only this time there wasn't going to be anybody to come and open the door. Not anybody she wanted to see anyway.

She remembered her father's shadow, falling across her in the streak of light from the open door, and the dark bulk of him before she was quite sure it was her father. Then the wonderful feel of his legs when she threw her arms around them. But there had been that moment when she wasn't sure . . .

Stop it, Sara, she told herself. Get up and do something. Finish the boxes. Finish that, at least.

What I must do, she thought, is get all Howard's things together in one box. Then I can call the Goodwill or the Salvation Army or the Welfare. I should do it now.

She was folding the fishing jacket and placing it with the other clothes when she remembered the time she hadn't known who Howard was. It was the night he came back from the coast unexpectedly, the fur coat in a box in his arms—he'd brought it that way on the plane—and she'd sat up in bed and seen him in the bedroom door and screamed.

There was a part of her that had known it was Howard, just as a part of her had known it was her father in the corncrib door. But the other part screamed. The other part was the uncertain, the never sure, the fraidy-cat Sara who she was now going to have to live with alone for the rest of her life.

She sat looking into the depths of the box containing Howard's personal things and another thought, tangible as the fishing jacket she had just neatly folded, came to her. *There is something else that I had just as soon not know. That is Moira's handwriting in the front of that book.*

Chapter 8

She picked up the book gingerly as though it were an unknown substance that might maim, poison, destroy, and held it in her hand, her eyes shut.

I wish I hadn't thought that, she said. I wish whoever or whatever is putting these thoughts in my head would stop.

But the thought was there. The handwriting was too familiar, too well known. It was Moira's, bold, black, inexorable.

All her life there had been the one thing—no, the two things—to hang onto. She might be only Sara, unimportant, untalented, unsure. But one man had been hers and faithful to her. One woman had been her friend. If what was in her mind now were true, neither certainty existed. Which made her whole life as ephemeral, as insubstantial as that of the crystal mouse, now gone as though he had never existed.

But, of course, it isn't true at all, she thought. It simply can't be true. I'm crossing that line between reality and unreality again.

But the voice was unrelenting. If it isn't true, wasn't true, it said, why did you have to have that crystal mouse in the first place?

Then the whole day came back to her, as a part of her had known it would do since she'd remembered standing in front of Dayton's window. The day she'd wiped from her mind as completely as though it had never existed. And how many other days? the voice said. How many others have you managed to ignore, forget, erase, by the same process?

Only the one, she answered. Surely only the one. That one is quite enough.

Howard had been apologetic about the trip to the coast. He hadn't wanted to go at all, but she'd insisted. The trip was, as most of his trips were, a trial trip, a testing. If he succeeded in the business on the coast there would be the raise, the promotion, the bonus. There had been no choice about it.

She'd known she'd hate it, but she'd known she could endure it. She'd behaved very well. She had put him on a plane to cross the continent and driven home to relieve the baby sitter, to sit alone and watch the snow begin to fall outside.

Then the long days began. The first day he'd called from the hotel. They'd talked about the weather in California, unbelievably hot and blue while Minneapolis cowered under the first heavy snow.

The next day she'd called Moira and hadn't been able to reach her. All day.

The nights were long, but there was Howie, warm and cuddly in the dark with her. The days were longer, but she hadn't had a full-time maid then so there was plenty with which to fill them.

The snow kept falling and the thermometer kept dropping. Howard called now and then; Moira was never at home. After a while she had begun to feel isolated, like someone in a cocoon, tucked away in the warmth of the house while snow covered the world outside.

It was not unlike her present feeling; the line between reality and non-reality had begun to blur. So that, when she talked to people—the postman, the cleaning woman, the man at the market—it was no longer the real Sara participating in the inane conversations. The real Sara talked babytalk with Howie, and tried to reach Moira by phone, and one day ran into a mutual friend who told her that Moira was on a business trip to New York.

Gradually the two Saras came to have their own duties and activities. The real Sara cleaned house until it shone and cooked small dishes of the foods Howard didn't like, and read romances from the lending library. The real Sara placated the dark gods of night by plans for foiling robbery attempts and made herself a coconut cake, which Howard didn't like, and ate it all with pots of coffee.

The other Sara told the cleaning woman that she was managing very well without Mr. Hillstrom and that he would be home soon. The other Sara called dutifully, but not hopefully, to see if Moira had returned. The other Sara thought of visiting her parents, but knew the real Sara didn't want to drive alone in the snow to the isolated farm.

Both Saras would sometimes merge to stand staring into the mirror, wondering if she was still pretty. Both Saras hugged Howie for comfort, and once they went together to a movie late in the afternoon, coming out into artificially-lit streets where the snow was pushed back from the walks in dirty heaps and people bundled to the eyebrows made cheerful sounds in the Minnesota night.

She walked along the cleared sidewalks, looking into windows, wondering whether to take a bus home or splurge and get a cab. Then on a busy lighted corner she had been shoved against a building by a hurrying man, running in worn shoes and a thin, shabby coat through the darkness, disappearing into the early-evening crowd. In a sudden panic, as though the rushing stranger had identified her for some strange purpose of his own, she had hailed a cab frantically and been driven quickly home where the baby sitter had looked at her in mild surprise and asked if she were ill.

She had been ill, but only because she was frightened. She'd tried immediately to call Howard only to have the hotel operator tell her she couldn't reach him because he'd left word no calls were to go through to his room.

For long frustrating moments she'd tried to argue with the operator, only to be told finally and firmly that she—the operator—couldn't help if she *was* Mrs. Hillstrom, she had her orders and that was that.

She hung up the phone in a rage, shaking, and at last beginning to cry in the emptiness of the apartment, so loudly that Howie had wakened and begun to cry too, adding to her panic and frustration.

She had picked him up and wandered around the apartment, hugging him and muttering to herself that if he were ill or injured it would be impossible to reach his father.

After a while he had gone to sleep in her arms and she'd tucked him back into his bed, spending the rest of the long night alternately trying to reach Howard and going to the crib to look at Howie's peacefully sleeping face.

When she did reach Howard at noon the next day he'd said it had all been a mistake, that the message he had left was for his calls to be transferred to another room, that of a business acquaintance with whom he was having a few drinks. He'd been first amused, then as she persisted in telling him her fears and misery, annoyed, exasperated, and finally, angry.

"Should I just forget my job, the whole works, and come home?" he'd said.

What must surely have been the other Sara told him as far as she was concerned he could go to hell.

He told her then that she was completely incompetent, and that had such a ring of familiarity she was grateful for it. But she hung up on him anyway. And waited ten whole minutes before she called him back and apologized.

I was always apologizing, she thought now. Always. And for what? Because *he* felt guilty. That's for what.

She looked down at the book in her hand. How long had it

been in her house, in her life? Hidden away in a box along with all those other things, as though they were somehow shameful too: Howie's letters, her picture in a bathing suit, a set of silver-backed brushes. It made no sense. But the book itself made sense. Just as everything had made sense to her that long-ago day, walking the streets of the city after Howard had returned with the mink coat in a box.

At first the coat hadn't mattered one way or the other. She had been so glad to see him after the initial moment when she hadn't been sure it *was* him in that dark doorway, to know that all the long dead lonely days were over, gone with the California sunlight she imagined still on him, that had most definitely tanned him so that he was almost a stranger to her. She hadn't even noticed the box until he'd thrust it into her arms.

"Times are looking up, girl," he'd said. "All went like clockwork, and the promotion's on ice. The coat is just the bonus money. Now aren't you glad I went?"

She had been. It wasn't until the next day, when he'd gone to the office to make an early report and she'd picked up the phone to call Moira, that she'd had other thoughts; the thoughts that sent her out into the icy day to the department store window.

Moira had been there. After all the days of an empty ring in an empty apartment the phone had been picked up on the first burr and Moira had said, "Hello, darling. How marvelous to hear you. I just got in last night."

"Did you?" Sara had said happily. "So did Howard. I guess all my life is back to normal again."

Moira hadn't said a word. There had been a long wire-humming silence finally broken by Moira's laugh. "Oh Sara," she'd said belatedly. "There's no one in the world like you."

And Sara had thought, She's patronizing me.

Never, in all the years Moira had been her friend, had it occurred to her to wonder why she was her friend. Why exciting, interesting Moira with her career and her men and her marvelous life should remain friends with mousy Sara. But now it did occur to her. And with the thought came other thoughts, crowding between her and the bright voice on the phone.

She didn't dare mention the coat, and she hung up as quickly as possible, though there had been no way on earth to keep from making a luncheon appointment with Moira. Moira knew it was Mrs. Clemons' day at the apartment. Moira knew that Howard would have gone straight back to work.

"Don't say you can't come to lunch," she'd said. "I know perfectly well Howard went right to that office. He wouldn't take a day off for you, me, or the Virgin Mary."

And Sara had had to say, All right, thinking, But what a funny thing for her to say.

After she had dressed and given Mrs. Clemons the instructions about Howie's lunch she'd stood indecisively for a long moment before deciding to wear the coat. After all she couldn't hide it forever. If this thing she was beginning to fear had happened to her there was no way out. Sooner or later she would have to appear before Moira in the coat, the coat that even she, dumb Sara, knew was as often construed as an apology from an erring husband as a present for favors received.

Wouldn't it be funny, she thought, shrugging into it, if Moira had one on too?

Looking back on that thought, she realized it was as errant as the thoughts that had been plaguing her now in these lonely days. Maybe someone had always been telling her things in an acerb language. But she had only listened when the need was great.

The restaurant had been bright and warm after the cold streets, but she'd kept the coat on rather than check it, shrugging it off at the table and sitting on it.

Moira had been late, as always, and she'd waited nervously, telling herself that she was still under the spell of the lonely days and that nothing was, or could be, the matter.

Then Moira had come, turning heads, as she always did, striding toward the table, smiling at Sara. And Sara had seen that she had a suntan as deep and unnatural to the Minnesota winter as Howard's.

Moira had leaned over to kiss her cheek in the familiar gesture of all the years of friendship, sat down, ordered her martini, and said, "What's the matter, Sara? You look peaked. Surely you aren't pregnant again."

She wouldn't have said that if there had been anything, Sara thought. She couldn't have said that. But, of course, she could have. It was only Sara who couldn't have under the same circumstances, and Sara would never have been involved in that sort of circumstance in the first place.

She tried to smile. "Hardly," she said. "Howard just got home last night." She paused. "You look good, Moira," she said. "You look just great."

"It's the tan," Moira said. "I guess I might as well confess. I haven't been in New York at all. I've been in Miami. Where, let's face it, I shouldn't have been, but where I had a glorious and never-to-be-forgotten time. But don't ask me about it. You know."

Sara had clutched her glass of sherry, and tried to look interested and uninterested at once.

"What are you going to eat?" Moira said. "I'm famished. I think I'll have to have the steak. You too. It's on me."

Sara could still taste that unchewable steak which she had tried valiantly to swallow. She could still see the sea of dimness the restaurant became in front of her, with the white-coated waiters scurrying between tables, the murmur of conversation buoying them up in the gloom like an invisible inflatable mattress.

She had smiled a lot and listened and nodded. She had reported on Howie's progress and Howard's bonus. She had said she'd seen a movie and baked a cake.

Then they were standing to go out into the sunshine and Moira had seen the coat.

"My God," she'd said. "He didn't."

Sara had raised her chin defiantly and said, "Why shouldn't he?"

"I just didn't know he was doing so well," Moira had said. "I'd no idea. I guess the trip to the coast paid off, what?"

"I guess it did," Sara said.

Outside the sun had been like bright needles glancing off the snow. Moira had put on her sunglasses. Sara had never gotten accustomed to wearing them. She never did until they moved to Florida. But she had wished she had some then. To hide her eyes too.

She stood there in the heavy coat, feeling weighed down by all those murdered animals, feeling as though each skin might sprout its original teeth and gnaw at her vulnerable skin.

"It's really magnificent," Moira said.

"Thank you, Moira," Sara said.

After Moira had walked away from her, striding through winter snow with her flamboyant tan, Sara had walked for a long time, staring unseeingly at the people who passed her, at the dirty snow in the gutters, at the crowded shop windows, at the high empty sky.

When she focused again on an object it was the crystal mouse in the window, cunning yet majestic on his bed of black velvet.

As though the sight of the mouse had called forth the thought the walk had suppressed, she felt it with a pang of physical force, as though someone had socked her in the solar plexus, and her mind was able to articulate it. Howard and Moira had been together on the coast. It was a terrible thought, but strangely, one she could live with. The one she couldn't followed: Howard had decked her in the skins of perfidy for Moira to crow over.

She looked at the mouse and he looked back at her.

It simply isn't true, he seemed to say. *Nobody is ruthless enough to do that to us, Sara. Us, the vulnerable, the unde- fended. They poison us and set traps for us and the very ruthless might knock us in the head. But they do not plot and plan per- fidious and hideous punishments for us. We simply aren't worth it to them. The strong do not use their subtle weapons on the weak. They use them on each other. We are, at the least, safe from that.*

With gratitude she had gone into the store and purchased the mouse, which had cost far more than she could afford, even with the promise of Howard's promotion.

The box had been silver and tied with a gay ribbon and she had carried it carelessly, a finger through the loop of twine, swinging on her gloved hand. A present. From Sara to Sara. With love.

At home she had set him on the coffee table, admired him, then transferred him to a more permanent position of honor atop the one piece of really decent furniture in the apartment, an old secretary that Howard's mother had left him.

With his presence, small, shimmering, indomitable, she had been able to say No to all her suspicious and paranoiac thoughts. She had been able to live with Howard, with Moira, with a mink coat. She had found a modicum of courage, dignity, self-belief that had allowed her to live again as Sara, mousy, but not cringing. Not pitiable, not despised.

And, now, the mouse was gone.

But a memory, forgotten, abjured, had come back to live with her. A book of poetry, signed in a bold black hand.

Dammit, dammit, Sara said.

She put the book back into Howard's box. She stood, went to the black expanse of balcony door, opened it and stepped outside. Below her the round lights reflected from the swimming pool. By leaning over the balcony rail and peering down she could see the pool's flat surface, undisturbed by any alien presence, a body of water in the dark of night. It had no message for her at all. She went back inside and closed and locked the balcony door.

You haven't looked in the closets, the voice reminded her.

All right, I'll look in the closets, Sara said.

She took the one in the bedroom first because it was the most difficult; filled with clothes, crowded with shoes and bags and hats. But no crystal mouse was there. There was Howard's indiscreet Florida suit; there were Sara's sandals and pumps and sensible walking shoes; there was a frivolous hat of flowers worn once to an afternoon tea; there was the unbecoming yellow dress.

She closed the door and chose the linen closet. Towels and washrags and bathmats that matched; a limp and ugly douche bag on a brassbound hook; sheets and pillowcases and an electric heating pad; two laundry bags and a box of stale sachet.

The pantry revealed the paltriness of life alone, the scanty supply of cans and boxes and tins of a small existence. Tea towels in neat clean stacks.

That left the closet in the hall. The hall closet of comedy and congestion. The place where everyone shoved the unwanted, the undefined.

She opened the door and stared at the coats on hangers, the boxes underneath. She pulled the boxes out. She felt, with trembling hands, through the pockets in the coats. At last, in an inexplicable mood of defiance, she pushed the coats aside and looked at the back of the closet. Where . . . with a sudden and intense, though completely unreal sense of horror, she found herself gazing into the still, white and silent face of Moira. Moira, dead and yet alive behind the coat-closet coats.

She screamed. And as the dead eyes looked with no compassion into her own, screamed again.

Chapter 9

Crouched against the wall, facing still the revealing mirror she hadn't yet admitted was a mirror, she was crying. She cried for a long time into the unrelenting hours between midnight and dawn.

At last she made herself stand up. She felt cramped and sore, and she wondered how long she had sat there, huddled against the wall, staring unseeingly into the closet.

Certainly her own image now held no particular terror. There was only a no-longer-young woman in a wrinkled dress with tousled hair, gazing back at her. She could not recapture in these moments of coming dawn the shock and horror that had accompanied that sudden glimpse of a woman staring back at her from the back of the closet. It was the sort of thing that would have been funny . . . once.

She had completely forgotten putting the mirror in the back of the closet. It seemed ages ago when she had done that, though it was only during the first days of moving into the apartment, really only a week ago.

It was an ornate, full-length mirror with wooden carvings of birds and fruit on the frame. She had picked it up in one of Cape

Haze's consignment shops when she'd discovered the only mirror in their rented apartment, with the exception of the medicine-cabinet mirror, was a blurred and badly hung mirror in the small bedroom. For years it had hung on the inside of the closet door in that old apartment. They simply left it when they went back to Minneapolis and no one had ever removed it during their absences, probably believing it to belong to the apartment, in spite of its incongruity with the maple and chrome of the regulation apartment furniture.

When she'd surprised her image in the closet last night it had been as though she'd never seen a mirror, or her own image. But even now, after the shock and the remembrance of shock, and the hours of misery that had followed, she was filled with a strange surprise that she could possibly have mistaken her own image for Moira. It was as though she'd taken a mouse for a Persian cat. As strange as if she'd thought of herself as pretty young blond Sara.

She reached into the closet and turned the mirror around and pulled the coats back across the rack. She shut the closet door.

Feeling as though she were climbing a mountain with every step, she went into the living room and across to the balcony doors. Opening them, she could hear the sound of birds heralding morning. Already there was a lessening of darkness, as though the atmosphere itself had lightened in preparation for actual light. The globes of light around the pool still burned and she was gratified to find they actually stayed on all night.

She stood on the balcony, holding the damp cold railing with both hands until the first streaks of light came into the sky. Then she went inside and showered and got into her nightgown and into her bed. She set her alarm clock for ten. She could not let herself sleep past then; it would make for a bad start to another day.

When she woke, a few minutes before the ringing of the clock, she felt refreshed, normal, healthy, and slightly ashamed of herself. She also knew exactly where the crystal mouse was.

136

She didn't go immediately to the place. Instead she made coffee and toast and took it onto her balcony to breakfast in the Gulf light, watching the waves rolling from the sand bar in to the beach. She dressed in a linen dress and carefully made up her face. She made her bed and washed her few dishes.

It was only then that she took the empty pasteboard box off the garbage can, removed the lid, and after spreading a paper sack on the floor, began to go carefully through the garbage.

He was about halfway down in the scant coffee grounds, tea grounds, and wads of paper packaging that had found their way into the can during the last three days. He was in two pieces, the head neatly severed from the body as though with the precision of a guillotine. Except for the simple break he was completely intact. Even to the fragile whiskers.

She washed the two pieces carefully under the faucet and set them on the drain board. The only thought in her mind was that she'd have to get some epoxy and repair him. The break was smooth enough so that she should be able to handle it herself.

She got her pocketbook and went out into the empty corridor. Automatically she tried the door next to hers and found it still locked. Then, in a sudden compulsion, she walked along the corridor past the elevator to the two back apartments. The door of the first one was firmly locked. But the door of the second, further down the corridor, gave under her touch, just as the one of the apartment next to her had on that terrible night. She stood for a long moment before she pushed it open and went in.

Unlike the apartment next to her own, this one was furnished. She was standing in the middle of someone's tastefully appointed living room. Bright abstracts looked down from the walls, a black sofa sat before a white rug. Small blue vases sat on the mantelpiece.

"Hello?" she said hesitantly, but she knew there was no one there.

She crossed the room slowly and looked out the balcony doors, opening from the side of the room to take advantage of the Gulf. Two butterfly chairs sat on the balcony. The balcony doors were locked.

Peeping into the bedroom, she saw a French provincial bed covered with a spread of peacock colors, an appointed dressing table, an ormolu clock on a marble stand. In the kitchen there were dish towels in a Rousseau print.

She backed quietly out of the apartment and pulled the door to behind her. This must be the apartment belonging to Mary Appleby's friend who had gone to Europe. But why was it open? She stood for a long moment outside the white door, not thinking of anything as she stared at its featureless face.

It was dark in this back corridor; realizing it, she hurried to the elevator and closed herself thankfully into the silent sliding box. Even the parking ramp seemed cheerful in comparison. She drove down the ramp and out into the sunlight.

Driving into town, she was surprised to see that the car needed gas. It didn't seem that she could have used a tank since the last fill, but then she wasn't at all sure of just how long that had been. She realized she wasn't sure how long exactly it had been since Howard died, how long since she'd moved into the Triton, how long she had been afraid.

She pulled into the first station she had a credit card for and let them look under the hood and check the tires and do all the things Howard always had them do. She signed the slip and put the receipt and the stamps into the glove compartment.

"Anything else, lady?" the attendant said. He was tan and young and cheerful, and he seemed to be looking at her with a quizzical expression.

She shook her head, wondering how much of the sleepless nights showed on her face.

He turned away, uninterested, and she drove on to an antique shop on the circle. They told her the best thing to use for glass mice and she came away with the small tubes of glue tucked into her purse.

She still wasn't letting herself think of anything at all. Instead, she drove across all the connecting bridges to the southern key where Mary Appleby's condominium stood. A man who could have been the double for Mr. Bishop sat at a desk in a lobby identical to that in the Triton. He buzzed up for Mary.

Surprisingly, she answered and Sara went up in the elevator to a corridor of the same grays and whites as her own, to knock on a white door also like her own.

"Darling!" Mary Appleby said. "Come in. I was just going to have a pitcher of bloody marys and a salad. Your timing's just right."

"Hello, Mary," Sara said.

Standing awkwardly on the threshold of Mary's apartment she couldn't remember why she had come here. She still had nothing whatsoever to say to Mary Appleby.

"Well, heavens," Mary said. "Come in and sit down, or admire my view, or something."

"All right," she said. She crossed to the double doors, like her own too, and looked at the Gulf from this different angle. There was no sand bar here and the waves banged in harder. But below her there were people in and around Mary's pool: an old lady and gentleman in shockingly loud bathing suits lying in reclining chairs, a mother with two small children, a pensive teen-age girl anointing herself with suntan oil with the slow quiet movements of a cat licking itself.

Behind her Mary set down a tinkling pitcher.

"I think I got into your friend's apartment by mistake today," Sara said.

"My friend? Oh. The gal who's in Europe. How'd you manage that?"

Sara turned away from the doors and took the glass Mary held out to her. "A wrong turning in the corridor," she said. "All the doors are so much alike."

"Heavens, yes," Mary said. "Particularly if you've had a few little drinkie-poos. It's like those tract houses. You remember all *those* jokes." She drank from her glass, then frowned. "But why was it unlocked?" she said. "Or do you suppose the same key fits all of them?"

"Oh no," Sara said. "It was unlocked." Dear Jesus, she thought. That's one I hadn't even considered.

Mary was watching her over the rim of her glass. "I was kidding, Sara," she said. "You *are* nervy, aren't you?"

"Am I?" Sara said. "Maybe so. It is lonely over there."

"I should think so," Mary said. "How many people are in that thing? There really aren't too many here, you know. I get the feeling these condominium people are overbuilding. But then, it isn't my problem. I'm sure the hell not invested. Good old Last One just pays my rent."

"When do you suppose your friend's coming back from Europe?" Sara said.

"God knows," Mary said. "She's unpredictable. Maybe tomorrow, maybe six months. Maybe if I wrote her you'd moved in she'd come on back. Should I do that, Sara? If I can find an address."

"No," Sara said. "Certainly not. How silly, Mary."

"Well, actually, it isn't silly, Sara. There's no need to get on the defensive. Anybody could get spooked alone in one of these things."

"I bet you wouldn't," Sara said.

"I bet I would," Mary said. "Of course, my solution would be to find a boy friend. Fast. I don't suppose you'd consider that."

Sara tried to smile. "It's rather short notice," she said.

She was beginning to feel uneasy. She had never told her problems to other people, not even, she realized, Moira. Doing it now seemed to make her situation really hopeless. The thought of Mary Appleby knowing she was alone and frightened in the Triton at night made the fact all the more frightening.

"I'm not really afraid," she said. "Just lonely. I suppose any widow has to get used to that."

"God yes. Men are impossible, but after you've had one around nothing ever has quite the flavor without one. It's terrible, really. When they're there you want to shoot them and when they're not you want to shoot yourself." Mary poured from the pitcher. "Time helps though," she said in a surprisingly friendly voice. "And old devil rum too."

"I'm not sure about that," Sara said, and bit her lip because that was revealing too.

"And coffee and cigarettes," Mary went on. "And long lunches and traveling. You ought to consider that, Sara. You ought to go and see the world."

"I might," Sara said. "Someday."

"Now," Mary said. "When you need it."

"I can't afford it," Sara said.

"Nobody can afford anything," Mary said. "You just have to go on and do it."

"I suppose so," Sara said.

Sitting on Mary's sofa, in an apartment she didn't have to consider as a place of hidden corners and closets, watching the Florida sunshine across the neutral carpet, she felt completely unreal. More so than in any of the panic-stricken moments in her own apartment. She was solving no problems, helping nothing. She was merely trying to pass some of the minutes of time left to her before going back to the now all too familiar night. The blessings of daylight companionship were now a closed book. They were useless to her. She stood up to go.

"But aren't you going to have lunch?" Mary said. "I told you. I have an enormous salad all fixed. No problem. I'll just bring it out."

"I have to go to the damned dentist," Sara said, hoping the damn made the clichéd excuse sound more plausible. "It's always something, isn't it?"

"One damned thing after another," Mary said cheerfully. "How about dinner?"

"Not tonight," Sara said. "I'll still be full of Novocain. I'll call you." She edged toward the door.

"How long before you would consider going out?" Mary said. "With a man, I mean."

"Oh, Mary. I can't even think about that yet."

"I thought not," Mary said. "But consider it."

"I'll consider it," Sara said.

She got out the door as quickly as possible and stood trembling in the hallway, waiting for the elevator.

Once downstairs and outside, she got into her car and drove to the end of the key where she knew there was a public beach. She parked close to the edge of the sand and sat looking out at the ocean.

The afternoon had progressed, but the sun was still high and the beach was full of sunbathers and swimmers. She looked out over them at the water, rolling in in gentle swells, the waves breaking a little further up the beach on each wave with the incoming tide.

The rest of her life, she believed, would be like the scene before her. The people would remain on the beach. What remained for her was beyond them, immense, uninterested, empty, and inexorable. Any intercourse with human beings was bound to be as surface-slick and unconcerned with the real self of Sara as these posturing people on the beach were to the ocean. Whatever it was she had to face had to be faced alone. She turned the car and drove back toward her own key.

In the shopping circle she stopped and bought a *TV Guide* and some magazines. She placed them on the seat beside her, their bright covers as slick and surface-seeming as her conversation with Mary Appleby.

As she waited for the light on the corner she saw among the people on the crowded sidewalk a familiar bright halo of hair, a certain walk. The light changed and she drove on, seeing from the corner of her eye the hand raised in greeting, hearing the mocking voice, "Hi, Sara, Hi, Sara," as she drove on past.

Looking in the rear-view mirror she saw that the girl had already vanished into the crowd in front of the Spanish restaurant.

If it hadn't been for the hailing voice she wouldn't have been sure she'd seen her at all.

The two-pieced mouse still sat on the drain board, his crystal pieces catching the rays of afternoon sunlight. He was dry now, and Sara set about mixing the glue on a small piece of cardboard. With infinite care she put the head back on the fragile body. She wiped him free of excess glue and placed him on the window ledge. She washed her hands and put away the mess.

The mouse seemed to regard her quizzically, not with the old sense of comradeship. She regarded him quizzically too. She still hadn't let herself think about whether she had actually broken him herself or not.

There was still the possibility of the TV men, an accidental elbow knocking him over and the subsequent concealment of the broken pieces. There was Mr. Bishop himself, who had most certainly broken a lamp and who could therefore be suspected of being capable of decapitating a crystal mouse. There was also still the possibility of person or persons unknown. There was always that possibility.

But there was also Sara. Who knew him best and who could quite easily have done it herself. Because Sara didn't trust Sara any more. Not after the shock of that mirror last night. If she couldn't trust herself it was sad indeed, for she had realized today that there really was no one else.

She knew she must form some feeling of solidarity within herself if she were to exist through the days and weeks and months ahead. She must build a personal fortress within this useless fortress in which she lived, something to keep out the unknown as well as the known that threatened to assault her from every side. To survive she would have to learn to live with the unexpected: vagrant laughs and clinks and broken crystal; empty corridors and silent rooms. That she might manage. But there were the crowded and unpredictable corridors and rooms within her mind. These, she knew, were quite likely to be the most dangerous of all. It was there the forbidden heads hung on the wall.

She opened her *TV Guide* and looked for a program to occupy that crowded mind, allow it to, for a little while at least, ignore its own crowded corridors. There was very little listed that appealed to her. But then, it was the summer rerun season. Perhaps, she thought wryly, I'm simply in the summer rerun season of my life.

It wasn't time to make supper so she settled herself in the living room with the magazines, thinking of that other living room she'd gone into this morning, wondering what sort of woman would have an apartment like that, admiring, almost furtively, the bold paintings that had hung on the walls. She wondered if she'd ever dare buy a painting like that for her own.

She had never liked modern art; but then she'd never liked country music before either. Perhaps now those bold splashes of color might cheer her blank walls. There were local artists, paintings could be purchased from them, and some of them, she understood, were supposed to be quite good. She knew nothing about it, but she could look for the cheerful ones.

Her mind roamed over the few paintings she could remember having seen and liked. Oddly enough, none of them seemed to have been cheerful at all. In fact, most of the ones that came to mind, imposing themselves between her and the bright pages of her magazine, were crucifixions. Certainly she didn't want a crucifixion on the wall. Not here. Not now.

She'd had a friend once who, though non-Catholic, was raising her son as a Catholic because her divorced husband had been one. During her working week she had boarded him with a cheerful Catholic Irishwoman who raised him along with her own brood. His weekends he spent with his mother in her small apartment.

One day when he was about four he'd wandered solemnly all around her apartment, looking at each room. Then he'd said to her, "Mama, why don't you have a God on your wall?"

The friend had told Sara this, laughing, and Sara had said, "What did you do?"

"Do?" the friend said. "I got a God for my wall. What else could I do? But I found one I could live with, a very old crucifix, carved from a marvelous piece of wood. I came to be quite fond of it myself."

I suppose, Sara thought, one can grow fond of anything.

Or come to hate it, for that matter.

She was thinking of the mouse. She knew quite well her attitude toward it was ambivalent. Which made it all the more likely she had snapped him herself in one of her endless, frightened circuits of the apartment. Except that she couldn't remember doing it at all.

But then she'd forgotten about putting the mirror in the back of the closet. At least, she hadn't remembered in the moment of first staring into it.

She got up impatiently and went to look out the balcony door. The afternoon was further advanced, but it was nowhere near night. Below her the blue of the pool gleamed and she decided to go down and sit on the edge of it.

She saw a mental picture of herself, looking relaxed and luxurious as the people had looked around Mary Appleby's pool. Perhaps if she began to behave as other people behaved she would, inadvertently, begin to feel as other people felt; secure, certain, contented, and unafraid.

She found her bathing suit, a simple black one-piece bathing suit, the only kind, she realized as she struggled into it, she had ever owned. She found suntan oil and her beach coat and her rubber flip-flops and a large-brimmed hat. She put magazines and oil in a beach bag, remembered cigarettes and put those in too. She stood at her door, attired for sunbathing, and tried to believe she was going down for fun.

Pressing the elevator button, she wondered what fun meant to her. She couldn't seem to remember when and if she'd ever had it. Would traveling, as Mary Appleby had said, be fun? As the elevator sighed her down she thought of standing in the Louvre and staring at crucifixions; of watching pigeons flutter over the canals of Venice, of seeing the changing of the guard, of looking in wonder at the ruins of the Parthenon. It seemed to her that in any and all of those places she would be hot and sticky and uncomfortable in a heavy suit; that she would be worrying about the language, the money exchange, the problems of transportation; the lettuce and the water and where to find the bathroom.

The elevator came to a stop and she realized she'd automatically pushed the button for the garage. She pushed it again for the first floor and was carried to the lobby. There was no one there. Perhaps Mr. Bishop was having his nap. He had to sleep sometime. She went through the empty lobby and down a narrow hall to the front of the building.

The pool waited for her, calm, blue, and empty. She sat beside it in a white-and-blue lounge chair and took off her beach coat. Out in the Gulf a boat went by, and she wondered if the people on board were watching her through their binoculars and thinking that she was a happy lady leading a life of leisure in the Florida sun. The sun was still hot and she could feel a faint film of perspiration on her face. She tilted the sun hat over her eyes and lay back in the chair.

Almost instantly she was dreaming. Howie and Ely were finding something on the beach. They were wearing white bathing suits and were tanned almost black. Then she realized they weren't wearing bathing suits at all, the white marks were only where they hadn't tanned. They were digging their feet into the sand and tugging at something, pulling hard, their muscles straining against the weight of the unwieldy object that lay half buried and which they were trying to extricate. The tide was coming in and their labors intensified, until finally, with an enormous plop, the object came up out of the sand, unbalancing them both so that they staggered back, stumbling. Well, shit, Howie said, quite clearly; and then she saw that the object was the young blond Sara, horribly bloated by the salt water, and quite dead.

She woke with a start that hurt her chest and felt her heart pounding. She blinked up into the sunlight. There was a halo around her field of vision and into it a face moved, grimacing. No, smiling.

"Enjoying the pool, Mrs. Hillstrom?" a voice said.

She flinched back against the chair, wanting to shut her eyes against the presence, knowing she didn't dare do it. She sat up.

"It's very nice, Mr. Snyder," she said to the young man in the white ducks with the soft-walking sneakers. "Very nice."

Her voice sounded dry and rasping and the repetition of the words sounded vaguely familiar to her as though it were someone else speaking. She made her mouth into a smile shape.

"I told Mr. Bishop you'd probably enjoy having it filled," he said.

"Where is Mr. Bishop?" she said, in what she hoped was a pleasant social voice, but which seemed to emerge as a croak.

"Probably napping," Theo Snyder said. "He's pretty old to be holding down two shifts."

"Yes," Sara said. "I'd thought that. By the way," she added— after all this young man was in charge of things in a way—"I was certain I saw some unauthorized person in this pool yesterday. But Mr. Bishop seemed to think I was imagining things."

"Well . . ." Mr. Snyder said. And she thought, And so do you, young man.

"There is a possibility of kids sneaking in," he went on. "There's a certain amount of vandalism in this town, surprisingly among the more affluent of the young people. When most of them have pools of their own, you wouldn't think they'd have to sneak into someone else's. But that's the way their minds work. Harassment, you know."

I know, Sara thought. I know all about harassment. You might say I'm getting to be an expert on it.

The young man's smooth voice was going on. "Something will have to be done if it is true. We certainly can't risk a law suit, and, believe me, if one of them so much as stubbed a toe that's what it would amount to. Trespassing or not, they'd sue us to high heaven."

"I suppose so," Sara said. Her voice was back to normal, she noticed. It sounded only weary now.

Theo Snyder was watching her with what in someone else she would have labeled concern.

"It won't be long till you have some company here," he said. "Mrs. Gresham should be in any day from Europe. And in the fall the apartment next to yours will be occupied by a doctor and his family from up north."

Sara thought there was a sly look in his eye. Nonsense, she told herself. You know he wasn't in that apartment. But he could have been in Mrs. Gresham's. It certainly was furnished and ready, right down to the peacock bedspread.

The sun was going down and Sara shivered involuntarily, even though it was still as warm as ever. "I guess I ought to be going in," she said.

"Nice talking to you," Mr. Snyder said and turned away.

Irrationally, she was annoyed with him for leaving, even though she had been annoyed with him for speaking to her. At least he was a human voice. But you've given up the human voice, she told herself.

She looked out at the sea, feeling in it a vast comfort, or threat. She stood up and, turning, gazed upward at the building towering over her, straining her eyes to see the top balcony, which was hers.

There was still a faint halo around things from the sun glare she'd slept in. The building seemed indistinct, an amorphous mass of white cut by blocks of glass, railings of black. She blinked and backed a step away, shading her eyes with her hand.

Just there, under the blue of sky, the black railings of her own balcony. She focused on it and started. There seemed to be someone standing behind the railing, a figure leaning out, looking down, a woman.

She blinked again, and backed another step away. There was no one there; only the black tracery of the balcony railing. She looked down, black spots zigzagging on the concrete at her feet.

She looked back up. There was only the building now, casting a shadow, tall and cold and gray in the evening light.

She went inside. The chill air fell clammily on her warm skin and the hallway was dark to her sun-struck eyes, so that she had trouble pushing the right button at the elevator. Mr. Bishop was still absent from his desk in the lobby. She didn't even feel very bad about that any more. She'd never really depended on him anyway. She went down the long corridor to her doorway, hugging her chilled arms inside the beach coat. She opened her door and went in.

Involuntarily she looked toward the balcony. There was nothing there, of course, except the iron furniture, which with each day seemed to become heavier and more ornate. She wished she had two butterfly chairs instead. But she had paid too much for the iron furniture. She couldn't just throw it away.

The room smelled faintly of the glue she'd used to repair the mouse. She crossed to the doors and opened them, letting some of the warm salt air into the staleness of the air-conditioned room. She turned away, then paused, wondering if the doors had been locked. She couldn't remember, even though she'd just that moment opened them. She stood still, knowing herself afraid to look over her shoulder. She sighed, and the sound was loud and omnipresent in the empty room.

She turned, and looked, and there was nothing there.

Nothing there, nor anywhere else in the apartment which she walked through now with the assurance of practice and searched quickly and quietly without even disturbing the surface of her mind.

Still, she thought, I'd feel better dressed. She went to the bedroom and shucked quickly out of the bathing suit and got back into her clothes.

The figure she had thought she'd seen on the balcony had been very indistinct. But it had been a woman. She didn't know why she felt so sure of that, but she did. It had been a woman. Just as the laughter had been that of a woman, just as that furnished apartment was that of a woman. All the half-seen, half-heard things were feminine. It was only the solid objects, Mr. Bishop, Theo Snyder, which were masculine.

The heads on the wall are always feminine, she thought. Even though it is masculine hands that have put them there.

She turned on her TV set because it was time for normal, masculine, Walter Cronkite, and she watched his confident face, though she carefully didn't listen to what he had to say. She wasn't required to listen to that. Loneliness was required. Fear was required. But not anxiety for all the strangers of the world.

After the news she rose to make her supper and saw that the globed lights around the pool had come on at their usual hour. She wondered briefly if they came on automatically or if that meant that Mr. Bishop was again on deck. She found that, for the moment anyway, she didn't really care.

In the kitchen, putting together her meager supper, she glanced from time to time at the mouse. From a distance his deformity was undiscernible. No one would know, unless they actually handled him or peered closely, that his head had been so neatly severed from his body. He looked quite as perky as ever, not even seeming out of place on the kitchen window sill. Looking, in fact, more at home than he had among his larger peers.

After supper and washing up, she flicked off the kitchen lights and went back to her television set, but the shows bored her and she couldn't even focus the surface of her mind on them. They didn't seem to possess the powers of attention-getting that the radio did.

Perhaps, she thought, it is because I've listened to things on the radio I never used to listen to, and these things on television have been coming into my living room for days and weeks and years. And they are always the same.

With a quick motion she flicked off the dial. But the silence was worse than the inane noise had been. She turned the set back on. It was as it had been with Mr. Snyder. She hadn't wanted his company, but she'd been annoyed when he'd withdrawn it.

She might be beyond human aid, but she wanted to know there were human beings somewhere, even if they had nothing to do with her.

She stood up, looked out the window at the globed lights, sat back down, leafed through a magazine. But tonight the pictures of bright objects, of expensive rooms, of expensive gadgets, rather than comforting her, made her feel pursued, inveighed against, urged to buy, to consume, to possess, to drown in objects.

She threw the magazine across the room and stood in a moment of silent horror at her own action. She couldn't remember ever having thrown anything in anger in her life. It was strangely satisfying.

Howie, when he had been small, had thrown things. Out of the crib onto the floor; bottles, toys, pacifiers. Later, when his manual skills began to develop, it had been his shoes. And there had been food. Sara could still remember the feel of a face full of slimy strained vegetables. Howie had never liked them. Once, furtively, she'd sampled them. After that she'd never tried to make him eat baby-food vegetables again.

She'd tried to tell Howard how bad they tasted. But that had been a mistake. He'd said a baby didn't have taste buds sophisticated enough to know the difference. But then the pediatrician had said a baby didn't run a fever when he was cutting teeth. And Dr. Spock thought you had twenty-four plus hours a day to be reasonable and explain twenty times and show by example. Howard and the pediatrician and Dr. Spock had never had to handle a live mass of baby with strong prejudices and principles and demands. Theories were marvelous. They made beautiful sense. They just didn't have much to do with reality.

Reality was never having enough sleep and only having so much energy. Reality was nerves strained to the breaking point by a yowl designed to do just that until you tended to whatever need was required. Reality was spinach in the face.

And shit too, that voice from nowhere said. Remember that, Sara. Sometimes he threw that too.

"And if he didn't throw it," Sara said out loud—and this time it was her own recognizable voice saying it—"he was certainly manufacturing it. With regularity and in quantity. And there was no one but you to dispose of it."

Oddly enough, the thought, rather than making her angry, amused her. She went across the room, smiling, and picked up her magazine and smoothed the ruffled pages and placed it carefully on the coffee table.

Tonight, for the first time, she hadn't been finding it necessary to look at her watch. She had, perhaps in the act of relinquishing human help, reached some kind of truce with time. Because time, after all, belongs to humans, she thought. She was surprised in the thought to see that the late news had already come on.

She watched the face on the screen and the pictures of devastation and confusion that flashed like lantern slides behind the measured words of the commentator. She watched, with more interest, the weather map with its high pressure system still holding rain out of Florida and the satellite picture showing clouds in other places. She thought that it would be nice if it should rain. The sound on the roof would be something cozy in this uncozy place. She always felt safer in the rain. It would be a hardy criminal indeed who would choose a pouring rain to come out in. She knew that all the scary movies said otherwise. But she wasn't living in a scary movie. Not yet, anyway.

While she waited for the old W. C. Fields movie to follow the post-news advertisements, she got up and went to the balcony doors, hoping to surprise a cloud in what she knew to be a cloudless sky.

She went outside and looked up, then down, seeing with the now-familiar pain in her chest that the globed pool lights, which had become a small, if remote, comfort, were not on.

She leaned over her parapet, but there was only darkness below her and the faint glimmer that, as her eyes adjusted, became the water in the pool.

She went back through the doors and with a firm step crossed to the intercom and pressed the button. Nothing happened. She waited a moment and tried again. There was still no comforting guttural voice. No mechanical thumps. No sound at all. She put her thumb firmly on the button and held it there for a long moment, imagining the buzzing sound going on and on into an empty lobby. She gave it up.

The panic came back then, as great and as detailed as on the first night of loneliness. All the careful thinking, planning, the deliberate casting off of human aid, was for nothing in this moment of isolation the failure of Mr. Bishop's answering voice gave her.

She had not realized how much she had depended on that small intercom box and the fat old man at the other end of it. She had thought she had known fear before. Now she was all fear. Pictures rushed helter-skelter into her mind: the old man lying dead on the floor of the little lighted lobby, or worse still, in the dark.

If the globed lights were out perhaps that was only prelude to a general going-out. Perhaps someone, with careful intent, was seeing that the lights all went out, floor by floor, one by one.

She began to shake. She thought of silent feet, crossing the lobby, entering the elevator, padding down the carpeted corridor to her door. She would never hear them.

She put her hand out to try the buzzer again and stopped, sweat breaking out on her forehead. What if whoever had done something to Mr. Bishop hadn't known she was up here, and, because she had pushed the buzzer, now knew? Perhaps they had turned the globed lights off for just that reason. To find out if someone in some apartment would buzz. And when they did . . .

She leaned against her front door, listening toward the silent hallway outside. The only sound she could hear was the pounding of her own heart.

Oh, God, Oh, God, she whispered. What am I going to do?

She could phone the police, but would they come? Would they think she was just some hysterical woman? And if they did come, could it possibly be in time?

But the door is locked, she told herself. The door is locked, and the chain is fastened. But just how strong and how heavy was that chain? For instance, if Theodore Snyder had turned off the lights and was coming here now he would have a key, and that thin chain would be all there was between her and whatever his mission might be.

Her mind threw up grotesque pictures now, pictures gleaned from newspapers and paperbacks and late-late shows, things that could be done to you by insane people, things someone like Theo Snyder and blond caustic Sara might do for fun and amusement, for diabolic sexual purposes, for unknown reasons or gains or needs.

She turned and rushed from the door to the balcony doors and locked them, knowing the gesture silly and useless, that danger lay the other way. She looked at the furniture and wondered if any of it was big enough to block the doorway, and knew that it wasn't. Only the furniture of older, earlier days was good for that, the highboys and sideboards of our mothers, not the flimsy makeshifts of a Florida apartment. Even her dining table wouldn't serve.

She began to cry, wishing that it would go on and happen, that no matter how terrible her fate might be it would be decided, done and over. That it would come now.

Through her panic, one clear thought fought to the surface. This is what torture is. Not the rending, not the pain, not the actuality, but the waiting. The endless waiting, the not-knowing, the possibility of anything.

She had to act. She couldn't stay here waiting for whatever was going to come. She left the TV sounding into the room and grabbed her purse and opened the door.

There was nothing in the hall. Gray carpet and muted lights. She fled to the elevator and pushed the button, not allowing herself to think of what might be inside it once the doors slid open. There was nothing.

She stepped inside and thought for a moment of staying there, pushing different buttons and riding up and down all night. Only someone, somewhere on another floor, could push the button too, and deliver her, before she knew it, into their waiting hands.

She began to pray for the sanctuary of the lobby, no matter who or what might be there. There was a chance, if only a small one, that she could run, past what waited there, and hide somewhere, run even as far as the highway and flag a car, duck around the building and run down the beach. She knew there was no hope of getting her car. She simply hadn't the strength to go into that subterranean garage. She hadn't even considered pushing the garage button. What if the lights should be off in the garage too?

The doors slid open soundlessly. Her eyes felt stretched and she was no longer breathing very well, but she forced herself through the doors and into the lobby, braced to run.

The lobby was completely empty.

There was a lamp burning on the desk and Mr. Bishop's paperback book lay face down beside the telephone.

She moved across the lobby carefully, placing each foot tentatively in front of her as though stepping over quicksand. No one appeared. Nothing happened. She reached a point in space where she could see out the front door and saw that the globed lights of the entryway were out too. She walked closer to the door and saw her own reflection in the glass, a distrait ghost, peering nearsightedly. She whirled around, but there was nothing behind her.

Panting lightly, she cut her eyes to left and right. She advanced toward the desk and leaned over and looked at the back of Mr. Bishop's book. It was a copy of Guinness' *Book of World Records*, which seemed to her so extremely unlikely it gave her the courage to tiptoe toward the community room and peer around the archway into its cavernous depths. It was, as far as she could tell, completely empty. The bulks and shapes of the sofas and chairs crouched heavily, but normally, in their corners, lit by one small lamp on a side table. The glass windows were squares of blackness. She took a deep breath and tiptoed across the empty room toward them.

"What in the god-damned hell?" a voice said behind her.

Everything drained out of her in a rush of shock and horror, so that she was not at all sure how she managed to turn to see Mr. Bishop, red-faced and swaying in the doorway, and to say to him in a steady voice filled with disgust and acerbity, "Why are the outside lights off?"

Chapter 10

In her room the television was still on. W. C. Fields was chasing a tire down a steep hill as only W. C. Fields could chase a tire.

The trip back up in the elevator had been anticlimactic. After the initial disgust with Mr. Bishop and his inebriated condition, she had known so surely that any hope of him as protector, guardian, knight, was impossible, she had not even thought of the return trip as daring. It simply hadn't mattered. Now, back in the apartment, all the familiar specters sat in the corners waiting for her to deal with them. After all, there wasn't anyone else.

He had looked so silly and bumbling, even sad, trying to articulate, to explain that the management had decided as there were so few people in the building it would be economical to turn off the outside lights at eleven. He had even offered to go out and turn them back on for her. She'd told him it didn't matter. It didn't. Whatever was waiting for her was perfectly capable of coming through paths of light, of bypassing drunken doormen.

She looked at W. C. Fields and he reminded her of Mr. Bishop. She remembered a scene where he had performed with a bent pool cue and she could imagine Mr. Bishop in just such a situation. In her mind she clothed him in Fields's top hat and waistcoat and let him fight her spectral enemies. She even smiled.

She sat for a while, watching the television, giving the ads the same blank attention she gave to Mr. Fields. After a while the station went off and she turned off the dial.

It seemed to her that there were several things she should have done, should be doing, but she didn't know what they were. Mr. Bishop's condition had made everything so suddenly normal she hadn't been able to readjust. She had dealt with him simply, firmly, easily, as she would have any public drunk, as she *had* dealt with public drunks, here and in Minneapolis, as she had dealt with Howard when he'd had a few too many, as once even she'd dealt with Moira.

And the dealing, the reasonable detachment, had made everything so ordinary, so day-to-day, that she had calmly come up to the apartment in the elevator, come into her room, resumed her seat at the television, with very little fear or panic left in her. She hadn't lingered in the corridor, nor forgotten to quickly lock the door, but that had been only a small apprehension anyone might have on their way through an empty building toward the security of their own door. It had had none of the dry-mouthed, heart-pounding dread she had felt only a little while before, here in her own living room.

For this reason she wanted another task to perform, another normal everyday act to retain this feeling of everydayness. Maybe, her wry new turn of mind told her, she should have stayed downstairs and dried Mr. Bishop out. Instead she had left him to his lonely bottle and his book of world facts. Now she wanted a fact to deal with herself.

She went into the kitchen, but even that place, which almost always yielded some chore for idle hands, was completely neat and shiningly clean. The only thing out of place was the mouse on the window sill, regarding her with bright eyes. And even he was repaired.

In the bedroom she picked up her bathing suit from a chair

and hung it behind the bathroom door. She turned down her bed. In the living room, she straightened the furniture and plumped up cushions. She looked around.

"My house is in order," she said aloud. The words seemed so terrible to her that she longed to mess something up, to create some chaos for her hands to remedy, to find some reason for living to prove her right to yet one more night of existence.

Mending. The thought came to her with joy. There was always some mending because she didn't like to sew. Howard had never been able to understand her aversion for needle and thread. He said it was out of character for her. "Sara can't bring herself to sew on a button," he would say, to friends, acquaintances, strangers. And there was always that note of faint triumph in his voice. Why? Sara thought now, as she had always thought then.

But now her particular lapse served at the time of need. She got her sewing kit from the dresser drawer and went through her clothes until she had a small pile of things beside her on the bed: a dress needing a hook and eye, a housecoat with a rip under the arm, a dress with a hem to be put back. She regarded the pile of clothes with a fond eye. They might not last the night, but they were a start. She tilted the lamp shade and threaded her needle and began.

After a while she realized it was so quiet she could hear the sound the thread made as she pushed and pulled the needle through the material. It was a sound she could not remember ever having actually heard before. How strange, she thought, that never in all my life have my surroundings been quiet enough to hear the sound of thread.

She cast her mind back, remembering her mother, sitting by the lamp, sewing interminably, it seemed, on some rip or tear in some garment. It had been very quiet in the house at those times, because her father was a normally taciturn man and her mother didn't talk while she sewed. She talked in her kitchen, and her garden, and on the porch at night, but not while she was sewing in the lamplight. Still, even that silence had not been intense enough to allow for the sound of a needle pushing thread through cloth. There had been the tick of the clock, and the rustle of her father's farm magazine, and the chunks of wood shifting in the fire, and the faint rustles of night life outside. Only in a hermetically sealed modern box could that kind of quiet exist.

No wonder she'd been able to hear a laugh and a clinking glass. Those sounds might have come to her from around the world. But she didn't want to hear them again now. She turned on her radio, and the bright voice of her Texas disc jockey came to her. But tonight he didn't seem to bring the cheer that he had before. He sounded almost melancholy. She sensed him alone in a bare barnlike studio with cement walls that dripped moisture, communicating through mechanical means with only one man somewhere unseen in a control booth. His communication with her was through mechanical means too, and from so many miles away as not to be thought of as communication at all.

As if to verify her impression, he had no live guests tonight, but played instead old tapes of interviews with what he always called the great and near great of the "Grand Ole Opry." Who are the "near great?" she thought. What a really dreadful thing to say about anyone.

She turned him off in the middle of a sentence and resumed her sewing, listening to that terrible pulling sound that seemed to grow louder and louder until she reached the end of her seam and snapped the thread and heard nothing.

Be quiet as a mouse, Sara; quiet as a mouse, a voice from very long ago out of a time she couldn't even remember said. *Be quiet as a mouse and something good will come to you.*

She tried to remember who had said those words, and where, and why. She could hear the exact tone, intonation, a whisper almost. But when was it? Who said it? And had she listened? Had anything good come of it? She didn't know.

There was no more mending. She gazed sadly at the pile of clothes and put them away.

She could write letters. Except that there was no one to write to. There was Howie, but she couldn't face that yet. She had phoned, and written the one letter about the funeral arrangements and the apartment she was going to move into. She had tried to say something comforting to him because she had had a feeling he was going to feel much worse about it than he would ever let her know. But it had been an inarticulate letter, and she knew it. She didn't have another one for him yet. Maybe she never would.

It occurred to her that she hadn't received any mail since moving in here. Had she forgotten to leave an address? But no, the manager of the old apartments knew where she was. It was just taking time to forward through the intricate maze of the post office. After all she really hadn't been here very long. Her newspaper hadn't started yet either.

She sat looking at the sewing kit beside her, trying to remember how long she had been here. She counted back, past tonight, past the opening of the swimming pool, past Mr. Snyder and blond Sara and Mary Appleby.

She had only been here three days. This was only the fourth night she'd spent here. She couldn't believe it. She got up and searched out her pocket calendar to confirm it. That was all. Three days. Not even a whole week yet, not the weeks, months, years it seemed. Not even time for the post office or the newspaper to have found her.

But time enough for someone, or something. Time enough for that. Time enough for anything or everything, like those lost hours in that long-ago corncrib. They had been long enough to turn the trusted figure of her father into a thing to fear.

She got up and went into the hall and looked at the telephone. But she knew there was no one to call. She had given up that hope this afternoon, even before she had realized Mr. Bishop and his intercom were a snare and a delusion. Mr. Bishop. She saw him in her mind's eye, grappling drunkenly with Mr. Snyder, with a hippie, with someone in the swimming pool. She didn't believe he could hold anyone off long enough for her to run. He was about as much use as one of those plastic men you blew up and sat in your window to fool prowlers. Not even that much use if you got close enough to smell his breath.

She thought of the warm feeling a drink could give you and actually debated joining Mr. Bishop, but she knew that was a snare and a delusion too. When she'd tried it she'd ended up with *Jesus Christ Superstar* and the sound of a mocking laugh.

I could make tea, she thought. Then I'd have the dishes to do up. But there would be so very few. If she'd thought to stock in staples she could have made a sticky gooey cake and messed up a lot of pans to wash, but she hadn't thought of that. How could she have known she'd want dishes to wash in the morning hours? Who would plan for that?

She was still standing in the confines of the hallway, and it occurred to her that she still hadn't finished with the boxes. There was still that. Her house wasn't entirely in order after all.

She had a bad moment about opening the closet door, but she managed, and pulled the boxes out without having to push aside the clothes and gaze at the back of the treacherous mirror. Though a part of her wanted to.

The boxes looked bulky and unwieldy in her small hallway and she was glad of the mess they made. She dragged them into the living room, enjoying the disorder they brought with them.

She took out Howard's old fishing jacket and sat holding it in her lap. It was one of the things she really should have given his brother. She wondered if she should make up a box for him. But, looking at the worn sleeves, she realized it might insult Jack. She'd hang it in the closet and save it for Howie.

Having the disreputable old jacket there with her newly mended dresses made her feel secure. One's house could never be in order with a thing like that hanging in the closet. The rest of Howard's clothes she stacked neatly in a box for the Goodwill.

She was left finally with the personal things. She took them to the sofa and sat with them on her lap, deciding that these, too, should be kept for Howie. She put them all away with her scrapbooks; the picture, the letters, the brushes, and at the last moment, the battered books from the shelf. A small enough stack, not enough to embarrass Howie and Ely when they had to sort through them themselves.

In the end she was left with the slim black book of poetry. A fishing jacket and a book of verse. The sum of a man's life. The two things his widow didn't know what to do with. She thought that it should mean something, but for the life of her she couldn't see that it meant anything. She opened the book.

The bold black writing stared up at her. *Bonjour et A'voir.* Moira's hand? She was no longer sure of that. It had seemed so clearly hers, the slanting lines so familiar she had thought it had to be Moira's. Now it didn't seem so. Moira's hand had been bold and black, true; but it had been slanted backward, and the initial letters were different.

But if it weren't Moira's? Had she been wrong all the time about the whole thing? Had Howard brought her a fur coat simply because he had the bonus? Had she sat tight-lipped and forgiving—self-righteously forgiving—for all those years for no reason at all? Had there been nothing to forgive? Was it possible the faint uneasiness, the barrier she'd felt with Howard and with Moira for all that time had been of her own making?

"I can't think that," she said aloud. *That is only part of all the terrible things this building is doing to me. It isn't true.*

If it isn't, the inner voice said, why did you break the mouse?

I didn't, she said.

Didn't you? her inquisitor said.

She got up quickly, dumping the book onto the floor, and went into the kitchen. The mouse twinkled at her from the window sill. She picked him up carefully, looking at the small clever face, seeing that face looking back at her through all the years he'd sat on her shelf, a symbol of betrayal, a small hard cold reminder, augmented by all the cold hard crystal fellows she'd placed around him on the shelves of the rest of her life.

She tried hard to remember breaking him, tried hard to bring to mind an image of herself breaking him. "I didn't," she said.

But even as she said it she felt the mouse slip from her sweaty hand to fall shattering into the sink.

She couldn't think. Her mind felt as dispersed and shattered as the mouse. A jumble of splintered glass that had once signified something cohesive and whole, now good only for the dustbin.

Somebody laughed, a gay tinkling laughter, the laughter of young Sara. But which young Sara? The one raised on a farm, of course. But then, that was both of them, wasn't it?

She backed away from the sink slowly until she came up against the kitchen wall. She shut her eyes. *Be quiet as a mouse, Sara, and something good will come to you.*

But it didn't, she said.

Didn't it? the inexorable voice said.

I didn't want it, she said.

The voice didn't answer her this time. She opened her eyes. Evidently she had finally satisfied the inquisitor.

I didn't mean that, she said.

There was still only the silence, stretching out now, until she could hear again all the poundings and gurglings and sloshings of her own body, the blood in the veins, the liquid in the organs, the breath in the lungs, the grinding of the marrow of her bones.

She fled into the bedroom and got into bed and pulled the covers over her head. But all the sounds of her own existence went on anyway, louder now under the protecting sheets.

She had to get away. She jumped up, completely unthinkingly, and ran from the room. But the murmurings followed her, into the hallway, into the kitchen, into the living room. She ran toward the balcony doors and opened them, but there was nothing that way. Nothing but the night.

She brought herself up short against the parapet, knowing with the one small center of reason left to her that she had come very close to launching herself off into the blackness below.

Something had saved her momentarily; but what? Perhaps the

sound of the sea, coming inexorably onto the sand, an all-pervasive soughing in the night, telling her the sudden drop onto hardness wasn't for her, sending her scuttling backward to the sanctuary of open doorway, into the confines of the apartment and across the living room as though ricocheted to come up against the outside door.

She didn't hesitate there, but kept going, opening the door and fleeing down the long gray corridor with more than the murmurings of her own body with her now. Now there was a chorus of voices, soft, muttering, indistinct, but separate, each one identifiable, each one whispering its own particular message into the empty corridors of her mind.

There was Moira, tapping a cigarette on a black-topped table, saying, "No man will ever tell me how to live." There was Mary Appleby, lifting a brimming glass, saying, "One simply can't live with them or without them. So what is one to do?" There was young blond Sara, saying, "I picked him for his money and then I loved him. Isn't that a gas?" And there was someone else, a young woman with a coronet of braids, writing in a slim black book of poetry, *Bonjour et A'voir.* And that was Who?

She ran, pursued by all the female furies who chattered like an aviary of birds, who laughed from disembodied heads on castle walls.

She realized that she had run past the elevator, but it meant nothing. There was only the gray carpet under her feet, the white walls enclosing her, the pursuit of all those voices, the flight from the moated, fortified castle of herself.

Someone had said that to her. He had said, "Oh, damn your virginity. It isn't all that important. It's not worth the moat and the portcullis—and the pots of boiling oil. I wouldn't take the trouble to put up a scaling ladder. Forget it, baby. Forget it." Someone an awfully long time ago. A friend of Mary Appleby's, at the only party she'd ever gone to at the lake. She'd never gone to another party with that crowd after that. She'd never dared. Because he might have been right?

No, she said now, still running. No.

She reached the place where she was going. The door opened under her hand. She closed it and locked it and put across the chain. She was safe. And all the voices had ceased, were left outside.

She went in to the bedroom and went to sleep under the peacock spread.

Chapter 11

She came very slowly into the consciousness of day. There was bright sunlight lying across the many-colored spread, there was sunlight on an ormolu clock, there was sunlight on the crystal-appointed dressing table. There was an overabundance of sunlight in her eyes.

She didn't know where she was but she liked it. It was a very lovely place, one she felt she had known for a long time but had unfortunately had to be away from. They had had her shut up somewhere in another room, a room of pinks and blues and wrought iron. This place, with its bold color and light, was the place where she belonged.

She felt very good, and she yawned and stretched and was surprised to discover that she was still in her clothes. She sat up in confusion, looking uncertainly around the bright room, realizing she actually had no idea where she was. She looked again at the ormolu clock, the dressing table. She had seen them before. They belonged to the lady in Europe, Mary Appleby's friend. But what was she doing here in the morning light?

She slid off the side of the bed and stood up, finding it difficult to feel frightened here in this cheerful room, but beginning to be frightened all the same, for it was coming back to her, the shattered mouse, the sounds of silence, the whispered pursuit down the hall. She had done it again, betrayed herself, gone out into the dangerous corridor, exposed herself. Was exposed.

In confusion she tugged at her wrinkled skirt, patted her disheveled hair. What if someone found her here? What if the lady herself came home?

She hurried, remembering to tiptoe, across the silent sun-filled living room to unlatch the door and tiptoe down the silent morning corridor to her own open door. It didn't bother her now in the sunlight that the door was open. She entered her empty living room, seeing the slim volume of poetry lying on the floor in front of the couch, the one item out of place.

She picked it up and looked at it, wondering how she could have possibly not known it, remembered it. She had given it to Howard on that weekend, the one—and only one—they had had together before the marriage. But why shouldn't she have forgotten the book? She'd forgotten the weekend, pushed it so far below consciousness it seemed never to have happened to her at all.

She remembered it now. It swam into the empty room with her in a wealth of detail; sight, sound, smell, and touch.

Rain on a brown spring sidewalk, rain dripping from newly-green trees. Exhaust fumes and the grinding of gears as the bus pulled away from the curb and left her clutching her overnight bag with her hair escaping in damp tendrils from its tight coronet of braids.

Howard coming toward her on the unfamiliar corner, his raincoat flapping against his trouser legs, taking the suitcase, his hand cold with raindrops.

The steep, narrow stairs to the friend's apartment, the musty carpets, the single bed. A lamp chasing darkness, rain on the windows, an unfamiliar glass of bourbon, sandwiches of thick Italian bread. Howard, putting clean sheets on the single bed.

Happiness. That is what the feeling had been. Happiness.

Arms holding her while the rain fell. And she cried. And he made her another sandwich, and said, "I'm sorry."

And she had said, "I brought you a present," kneeling beside the suitcase, finding the book and her robe, handing him the one, putting on the other.

It had rained all night.

And the next morning she had said, "I'm sorry. There's a bus at ten o'clock. I'm going to go back to school."

Had written *Bonjour et A'voir*. And gone back down the steep and narrow stairs.

Hello and Good-by she had written. And suddenly she knew it had been just that. That night had been the only thing they had ever really had. Because she had withdrawn it all, withdrawn it finally so far that she had been able to forget it entirely. He had brought the scaling ladder, had stormed the fortress. And she had drawn up the drawbridge, snapped shut the portcullis. Had said, No, you didn't. It didn't happen. If you want me, marry me. Marry me instead. *Bonjour et A'voir*, Howard. I'll marry you when you ask me, Howard. But *don't touch me*.

She stood in the middle of the room for a while, holding the book. Then she took it into the bedroom and put it carefully with the other mementos. Let Howie and Ely puzzle it out. Only they probably wouldn't have to. They would probably know exactly what it was. The thought amused her. But it didn't really interest her.

She went into the kitchen and realized she'd have to clean up the mouse before making coffee. She went about the task quickly and with no emotion, wiping up the last particles with a damp paper towel, flushing out the sink with cold water, depositing the shards in the garbage can. She made the coffee and drank three cups and smoked two cigarettes.

I have to hurry, she told herself. There's an awful lot to do today.

As though in answer there was a sound from her living room

and she went in to find a litter of envelopes on her carpet underneath the letter slot.

She picked them up and took them to the kitchen. Most of them were sympathy cards and notes, but there was a real letter from Howie and a separate one from Ely, something she'd never gotten before. It was a short, stiff letter, written in an immature round hand, but it pleased her as no letter she'd ever gotten before. Howie's was just like him, terse, tough, to cover the real emotion behind it, exactly what she had expected. Ely's she read again. It was not that it said anything in particular, anything different from the other sympathy notes and cards. It was the fact that Ely, who scorned the social amenities, had written it. She put it on her bedside table to read again later. The others she put on the small desk in the living room.

There was, in addition to the sympathy notes, a card from Mary Appleby announcing a luau to be held at her condominium. Scrawled across the bottom was a note. Come and plan to spend the night—Mary. She smiled. It was kind of Mary, but she had given up all that.

It occurred to her that if she opened her door the paper would be there. She opened it and there it was, a signal on the gray carpet. She took it in and glanced at the headlines before going in to take her shower.

Daily event followed daily event in a preordained and uneventful sequence. She dressed and had more coffee and glanced through the paper. She straightened her already straight apartment. She made a grocery list on the back of an envelope.

No random voices spoke to her, no hectic thoughts invaded the morning. Some crisis had been passed and the fever was broken. Sara Callahan Hillstrom emerged unscathed into a sunny day and drove her car past a hung-over Mr. Bishop with a carefree wave of her hand.

At the shopping center she lingered for a long time in the supermarket buying the ingredients for an elaborate Italian cake for which she'd had the recipe for years and which she'd never made. Then she went to a dress shop and tried on dresses until she found exactly the one she wanted, a dress, she realized, that reminded her of the dresses she'd worn in that long-ago time when she'd first met Howard. It was a white dress with a long waistline from which gores spread in fullness, giving her a long-waisted appearance she usually didn't have. She bought new shoes too, and, in a final burst of silliness, a set of white underwear trimmed in lace.

She would have liked to purchase a splash of color for her walls, but she knew an original was hard to select without looking and choosing so she settled for a print which she found in the little novelty shop on the corner, already framed and ready to hang. She made one other purchase.

She went into the bar where she'd met blond Sara, half expecting to see her in the gloom. But there was no one there except two old men in golfing clothes. She ordered a Scotch and soda, drank it slowly at a table in the corner, and had a sandwich for lunch.

Her day was unrolling steadily around her in small richnesses, mail, paper, shopping, a drink, some lunch, the thought of the cake to make when she reached home.

There were still no vagrant voices, no strangers appearing to unsettle her mind. Since waking in the strange room with the sunlight there had been no other strangeness. The memory of that night with Howard was, after all, only something she had misplaced and found again. She felt purged and clean. If she was also reluctant to examine her own thoughts and feelings, why that was a return to normalcy too. That was the old Sara Hillstrom, living a surface existence, free of neurotic impulses, thoughts, or actions. Free, because uninvolved.

Back at the Triton she put her car into its slot and surveyed the garage. It was still an empty cavernous place and she rolled up the windows against the gloom of it, but she didn't lock the door. She went directly to the lobby rather than on up in the elevator and spoke to Mr. Bishop in his desk chair.

"Good afternoon," she said, hoping her pleasantness would make up for the embarrassment he must feel after his performance last night. But he looked embarrassed anyway. He rose, mumbling that he would turn the lights back on tonight if it was going to bother her.

"Oh no," she said airily. "I just thought there had been a mistake. If you intended to turn them off it's all right with me."

Theo Snyder came through the front doorway. "Using the pool today?" he said.

"I thought I might," she said. "It's awfully pleasant out there, you know."

"Did you get your mail and paper all right?" he said.

"Yes, thanks," Sara Hillstrom said. "I almost believe I'm about to get settled in after all."

She turned away to the elevator, aware of the look of satisfaction exchanged between the two men as she took her leave.

It is all so easy, after all, she thought, opening her door and putting away her purchases. Let your mind work and it betrays you. Ignore it and life becomes a thing you can deal with. She hummed to herself as she went about mixing the ingredients for her cake. While it baked she affixed the plastic-backed picture hanger she'd bought to the wall she was sure wouldn't hold a nail, and hung her new print. She looked through her *TV Guide* and checked the programs she wanted to watch that evening. She iced the cake and put it in the cakebox. She put her other purchase in the place where it belonged.

She went down to the pool for a short sunbath, watching the ocean roll onto the beach and gulls dipping toward home as the sun went down. Back upstairs she changed into her new white clothes and had a drink while her chop cooked.

While she was engaged in these activities it did not occur to her that she was performing rituals. She would not have believed it if her aberrant voice, now silent, had suddenly informed her of the fact. She was simply being, for the first time since Howard's death, Sara Hillstrom, the person she knew and recognized, the person she had been able to live with through all the long years.

She ate her supper and washed her dishes. She sat in front of her television set and watched a situation comedy, a magazine, open to the long story, in her lap.

Somewhere underneath the cool, calm surface, she knew and understood it all; had known it since she woke this morning, a stranger in a strange bed. It was simply that what she knew she couldn't face; and survive. It was all there, nonetheless, under the ritual of the too-sweet cake, under the ritual of the newly-hung print, under the ritual of the little white dress and the purchase on the shelf.

She knew. The furies that had pursued her down the hall, speaking in their various and well-known tongues, were neither friends nor foes, neither new nor old acquaintances. They were simply Sara. Sara as she had been, could have been, should have been, wasn't, and was.

That was why there had been no real surprise on discovering she had forgotten about the book of poetry, had even managed to have forgotten the occasion that had provided it. That was the reason there had been no surprise about pretty blond Sara with her gift of the new Christ, nor about Mary Appleby and her outrageous suggestions, nor about the discovery that Moira's image was in the back of her closet.

All those images, all those voices, the laugh next door, and the clink of crystal, were Sara Hillstrom—Sara Callahan—Sara who never was, and never would be now.

The figure in the corncrib door might have been, was, anything you made it. But Sara, Sara always still as a mouse, hadn't made anything of anything.

If that long-ago boy on the blanket at the lake had put up the scaling ladder, if she hadn't slammed the portcullis, she might be Mary Appleby, hectic, addicted to too much alcohol, but ready for a luau, ready at least for that.

Pretty blond Sara from the farm she had been too, but she'd

never have searched out and married a millionaire only to love him enough to have to turn in the end back to that age-old Rock of Ages; to feel the nails herself instead of just the sound of hammer blows.

And Moira; Moira too. That part of her really dead, dead eyes in an ornate mirror. The career girl, self-sufficient, productive, and not at all the seducer of her best friend's husband. That only in the best friend's blinded eyes.

Sara Hillstrom sat calm and still in front of flickering pictures on a screen. The furies that were unlived Sara had gone back to their hidden room in the tower, nothing now but heads upon the wall.

I didn't mean to intrude on your secret room, Sara told them silently. Hang there in peace. I didn't want to know. I didn't want anything but the peace of days, my crystal pieces on a solid shelf. I didn't want to be an old snapshot, a silly message in a book of poems, a frivolous laugh, a broken mouse.

But none of this came near to reaching the surface. Surface Sara watched comic antics on the picture box, and during the commercials read a story about a bored housewife, and got herself a piece of calorie-laden cake when the news break came.

Fear had gone with the knowledge of whom she feared; both fear and knowledge conquered now by all the rituals performed through the long day and its dying.

At eleven o'clock she went to the balcony and watched the globed lights go off. The turning off of lights, the saving of electricity, was Mr. Bishop's ritual. Perhaps it kept something away for him.

The late movie on channel 10 was a romance; Ida Lupino suffering in her small-boned fragile beauty, with no hint of the good strong director in her face. But channel 10 wouldn't come in. The signal was too weak and the picture began to roll. Sara adjusted the horizontal, but then the picture was snowy. She fiddled with the set with a long patience born of many nights of trying to watch channel 10 movies. But finally the dialogue faded and that of another distant channel came in on top of it, and she knew it was no use. She watched the insanity of Ida Lupino spouting the words of some mad doctor in the Amazon for a few frustrated moments, then turned the channel.

On the stronger stations, talk shows were in progress. Sara didn't like talk shows. She switched back to Ida Lupino's face and the mad doctor's words.

The world turned black.

In that instant of complete blackness and silence, before her mind could connect the effect with the cause and know that the electricity had failed, all the specters of the hidden room rushed out and claimed their rightful place.

Fear, the ancient fear of the dark, possessed Sara so completely that she was not at all sure she wasn't in that corncrib of childhood, where night had come and no one had arrived to rescue her. The inconceivable had happened, and nothing in the universe existed as reality any more.

She began to run, in random circles like a bird fallen down a chimney into the enormity of a human room. Only there was no one to open a window, a door, to let her out. She fell across a footstool, blundered blindly into the glass doors, skittered away by instinct to the other side of the room.

She knew now who and where she was. A lone creature trapped in an alien building, a building with sixty-five apartments and innumerable corridors, a building where nothing worked because nothing could work without electricity. She couldn't see, she couldn't escape, because the elevators wouldn't work.

She fumbled at the door and opened it and ran into the black corridor. She felt her way down the hall and pushed frantically at the dead elevator button. She ran all the way to the opposite end of the hall and fetched up against the wall with a horrid knock that bruised her forehead and sprained her wrist. She ran down the back hall and back again.

Some moat of sanity in her battered mind told her that there was a stairway somewhere, that if, in the dark, before something happened, before some hand reached her, she could find the stairway door she might yet be saved. She might yet find her way down the maze of steps into the world again. Because, if she didn't know where the stairway was, her pursuers wouldn't know either.

Slyly now, she slowed her own panic, forced her body to stop its unfocused flight, forced her heart to slow, her mind to work. She began to feel secretly and silently along the walls in the darkness, stopping to try each door she came to, finding each one shut against her.

Panic returned to slow her, impede her progress, turn her around in her own mind so that she was retracing her steps, fetching up finally at what she knew to be her own door only because it yawned open into more blackness. She almost fell through it when she put her hand out; then caught herself, both mentally and physically, and turned and oriented herself again in the darkness, beginning again the slow steps down the dark corridor, a mouse in a maze, hoping only for the door which, when bumped, would swing open onto freedom.

She found it finally, after she didn't know how many minutes, hours, ages, of slow creeping, of sudden spurts, of endless reaching out. Something gave under her tentative hand, a swinging door. She knew where she was now, at the end of the storage corridor where there was normally a red exit light, where, at any other time, she could have walked unerringly, where now, in darkness, it had taken a good part of the rest of her life to reach.

She pushed the door open carefully and cautiously and felt in front of her, one foot at a time placed slowly in front of the other, until she reached the top of the stairs.

She reached both hands and grasped the handrail. Then, with infinite care, stopping on each third step to listen, she made her descent.

Sometimes, in that endless time of creeping downward, she was sure she heard it, the sighing open of the swinging door, or of *a* swinging door; for who knew how many doors on how many floors she had passed, though she was trying to keep a certain count. She had gone down ten steps, then a turn, then ten more. So one floor, and then begin again. She counted, and counted again, and once she checked by hunting along the wall and finding the swinging door for—which floor?—she thought the eighth— at just the place it ought to be.

At one point—between the fifth and fourth?—she had had to stop and sit on the stairs, huddled against the wall, trying to keep the count clear in her mind, trying to listen into the blackness and silence for a following footstep. There she had known, with a sudden sharp stab of horror, that the footsteps could be coming either way. Up or down. Or both. She could no longer depend on direction to escape. No longer do anything but creep, silent as a mouse, down step after step after step, into a well of night.

But somewhere, underneath consciousness, something counted for her, something told her that here, just here, should she put out her hand, was the door that would open into the foyer that opened into the garage. She pushed and a door swung open. She was in a foyer, not a corridor, because by feeling along the walls she found the doors to the elevator on one side and glass doors on the other. There was nowhere else that she could be. The garage was just outside.

Now, she panted. Now. I can get to my car and turn on the car lights. I can do it. I've made it. If only. The *if only* entered her mind in red foot-high letters. If only Mr. Bishop hasn't locked the door.

But the mouse-courage that had crept with her down those endless stairs came to her rescue. If he has, it said, I'll take my shoe and break the glass.

She pushed the door. It opened. Through it came the night wind, a blessed cool clean rush of life on her sweating face.

She was in the garage, no longer a place of terror but the exit toward freedom. For the first time she was glad hers was the only car in the empty space. She had only to feel her way forward to the other side, then walk, slowly and carefully, until she bumped into the car. She had left the doors unlocked. She would open the door. And there would be light.

She moved. She crossed the rough concrete to the wall. She turned and felt her way carefully and slowly toward metal. She bumped against the fender sooner than she had expected. She was elated, excited, transfigured. Saved. She felt along the fender, the hood. The door handle was firmly in her hand. She opened the door. And the lights came on.

There was a sudden blaze of illumination, a blinding, hurting light that seared her eyes, her face, her inmost being. The princesses of the tower swam together and merged and became the one figure, the one face in the car before her, sitting under the wheel, dark hair piled on her head, hands limply on the steering wheel, eyes in a wide shocked stare gazing into her own.

You, Sara breathed—to Moira, to Mary, to Sara, to Ely, to her mother, to herself.

There was a second, a blinding second, in which she grasped it all, saw it merged and melded, saw everything that she could have been raising a hand toward her from the driver's seat of the automobile; and she shrank from it, knew it to be the thing she ran from, knew it to be the thing feared and forgotten. Then, with a grinding pain in her chest, it all became part of her and she stopped running, stopped caring, and let it take her, kindly at last, with infinite ease and comfort, into a surf-sounding night.

Chapter 12

It had rained at the cemetery. Mary Appleby and Connie Gresham had stood together in the damp grass, trying not to look distracted by the drops that had become heavier and heavier as the young minister read the service. There had been an assistant with an umbrella, but he had hesitated about whom to hold it over, not being sure of the chief mourners, not wanting to offend.

"I suppose I'm elected," Mary said when it was time to strew the flowers. "As the brother- and sister-in-law didn't come."

"I'll do it," someone said. A small blond girl in a flowered raincoat had stepped forward and taken the wilted petals and strewn them into the grave. Then she'd taken some dirt and thrown that too, and Mary Appleby had raised her eyebrows at Connie Gresham.

The girl vanished into the rain, coming down harder now, and the two of them ran to the car and went as quickly as possible to a bar.

"Well," Mary said when the drinks came. She took off her hat and threw it into an empty chair and took a good long pull at her drink. "That's that."

"Oh, Christ," Connie Gresham said. "Something else for me to feel guilty about for the rest of my life."

"Nonsense," Mary said. "It might just as well have been you. The shock was enough to kill anybody. Both of you thinking you were completely alone in that damned garage in the dark, and then having the lights go on like that. Jesus."

"It was pretty awful," Connie Gresham said. "It was bad enough when they all went out just as I drove in and parked. But I thought I'd just last it out and sooner or later they'd get them fixed. I'd just remembered the flashlight in the glove compartment when they went on and there the woman stood. Christ. I'll never forget the look on her face as long as I live. Only . . . only . . ." She paused, looking puzzled. "There, at the end, after the first horror wore off, she looked quite different, almost as though she'd recognized me and was about to speak. I don't know how to explain it, but it was as if she'd been waiting to tell me something very important and was terribly glad I'd arrived in time to hear it."

"My God," Mary Appleby said. "Don't start sounding like that or I won't let you spend the night in that place. It did for Sara and I don't want it doing for you."

"I'm all right," Connie said. "I just feel bad about it, that's all."

"She was already spooked out of her mind," Mary said. "I could tell. That's the way it is with those mousy types. They seem so placid all along and then when they do go to pieces they do it with a vengeance."

"But I don't think she did," Connie said. "I've talked to Bishop and Snyder, and they both said it was a hell of a thing, that huge empty building with no one in it. They got spooked themselves. They said all three of them scared each other every time one of them walked into a room. And once she thought she saw someone in the pool and Snyder said he just today found out there *was* somebody there, one of the kids who hang around the beach. He caught him at it again and he admitted to having been there before. There was that business about the mouse too. One of the

TV men had broken it and Mr. Bishop said they hid it. Later he decided he should have told her, she probably thought it had vanished into thin air. There were enough reasons for the poor woman to be distracted. Alone, and with her husband just dead. I wouldn't have liked it."

Connie drank from her glass and lit a cigarette. "In fact," she said, looking pensively out the window at the rain, "I don't think I'm going to stay there alone. I'm going to a hotel until some more people move in."

"What if they don't?"

"Then I'll damned well take a loss," Connie said. "I don't feel the need to be brave for anybody."

"Well, me either, for that matter," Mary said. "I guess I should have persuaded her to stay with me. But, to tell the truth, she would have cramped my style. There was something about her, a censorious look."

"She didn't look that way at the end," Connie said.

Mary shrugged.

"I went to the apartment," Connie said. "Looking for addresses, you know. It was clean as a pin. There was a freshly baked cake on the table, and this beautiful print on the wall. Some goddess, I think. Kwan Yin? And she had the most beautiful crystal collection. Only right in the middle of it there was a china mouse, the one she'd used to replace the broken one, I guess. But it all got to me. She was trying so damned hard."

"Oh hell, we all try so damned hard," Mary said. "It's the curse of the sex. Who the hell do you think that girl was, by the way?"

"The one at the cemetery? I can't imagine. Pretty."

"Not a relative," Mary said. "There weren't any. I guess you can't blame the in-laws for not coming; they'd just gotten back from Howard's funeral. And it would really have been silly for Howie to try to make it. I promised him I'd get all the personal things into storage. I don't suppose there's much."

"There's the crystal," Connie said.

Mary ordered another round. "Jesus, what a bunch of mourners," she said. "Me and you, and Bishop and Snyder, a pretty girl, and those two old men. Who in hell were they, by the way?"

"I think one of them said he was the manager of her old apartment," Connie said. "I don't know about the other one."

"Well, that's about the crop when you die in Florida," Mary said. "Cheers, Connie. *Salud y pesetas.*"

"I still feel like hell about it," Connie said.

The other man at the cemetery had been the man who had bought Howard's Mercedes.

On